This book belongs to

Kendra Kandlestar and the
Door to Unger

Kendra Kandlestar and the Door to

Written and Illustrated
by Lee Edward Födi

Brown Books ⧫ Dallas, Texas

KENDRA KANDLESTAR AND THE DOOR TO UNGER
© 2007 Lee Edward Födi

Manufactured in the United States of America.

For information, please contact:

Brown Books Publishing Group
16200 North Dallas Parkway, Suite 170
Dallas, Texas 75248
www.brownbooks.com
972-381-0009

ISBN: 978-1-933285-83-2 (Hardbound)
ISBN: 1-933285-83-4 (Hardbound)
ISBN: 978-1-933285-82-5 (Paperback)
ISBN: 1-933285-82-6 (Paperback)
LCCN: 2007931923

Also written & illustrated by Lee Edward Födi:

Kendra Kandlestar and the Box of Whispers
Corranda's Crown

Find out more about Lee Edward Födi at www.leefodi.com

For my
brother and sister,
who helped make
storytelling
fun.

LIST OF CHAPTERS

CHAPTER 1

A Mysterious Visitor

This is a story about monsters and mazes, and what it means to be lost. If you have ever been inside a maze, then you know that they do a very good job of making you lose your way. They are full of tricks and turns, and if you're not careful, you will find yourself going in circles or headed down a dark road with no end.

There are still a few mazes left in our world—you may have found yourself inside one if you've ever wandered through a farmer's cornfield or visited a palace garden. But really, there is nothing very frightening about these modern mazes, for they harbor no fanged goblins, no slurping monsters. But if you so lose yourself in this story, you just might discover such an adventure.

Our tale begins long ago in the tiny land of Een. It was a wretched night—the whole sky crackled with claws of lightning and the dark clouds boomed with thunder. Now, the land of Een is a very small place, tucked between the cracks of here and there. A normal-sized person might walk right through Een and not even realize it existed—especially during a terrific storm when the only thing anyone really wants to do is get indoors and dry themselves by a warm fire.

Yes, to you or me, a storm can be quite a dreadful affair—but think of the tiny people of Een: to them, a raindrop could be like a bucket of water, a gust of wind like a hurricane. Of course, the Eens are a magical people and have been in the world for a very long time, so I suppose they know a thing or two about getting through storms. Some experts say that Eens are related to Elves because they have pointed ears and can talk to animals, but I have also heard that they are related to no one—that they are a strange race of people all their own.

Whatever the case, we will concern ourselves with one Een in particular: the tiny girl named Kendra Kandlestar, who, on this dark and shadowy night, was nestled in her bed inside her uncle's house.

Kendra was in a deep dream. Those of you familiar with Kendra's adventures will know that this girl has had her fair share of dreams—many of them quite frightening. But this dream was pleasant. On this night, Kendra was dreaming about her family, who had mysteriously disappeared long ago, when she was just a baby. Even though she couldn't remember them, it was quite wonderful for Kendra to dream about her family: her mother, her father, and her brother, Kiro. Inside that magical dream world, she could clearly picture them all together: picnicking on the banks of the River Wink or resting in the shade of the yew tree, where she now lived with her Uncle Griffinskitch. In her dream, everything seemed right. Everything seemed perfect.

But the dream was not to last.

Suddenly, Kendra bolted awake and sat upright in her bed. What had awoken her? A sound? A light? No, it was the darkness. It was *too* dark, even for a black sky raging with storm clouds. She tugged nervously at her braids. Tugging always helped her clear her mind. Kendra had seven braids in all, radiating out from the top of her head like the rays of a star, so she had plenty to tug at.

Something is out there, Kendra told herself. Through the wind and thunder, she could hear a strange sound. It was a grunting sound, as if someone were in terrible pain. Kendra sat still, frozen for several minutes, but eventually her curiosity won out over her fear. So finally, she crept to her window and pressed her face against the glass—but she just couldn't see well enough. Frustrated, she wrenched the window open, and instantly wind and rain billowed into the room. She brushed the waving curtains out of her face and leaned out into the rain.

She could see and hear more clearly now. She scanned the yard around their yew tree cottage. Suddenly the lightning crackled again and—for a split second—illuminated the yard. Then she saw it—or, more accurately, she saw its shadow. She caught the dark shape against the garden shed, but she could not tell who (or what) it was. The shadow only told her one thing about its owner: it was simply enormous.

"It's no Een," she murmured to herself. "No animal either; it's bigger even than a badger."

3

She could still hear it breathing, but now, she detected something else: the sound of it dragging itself across the ground, between the shed and the house. *Whatever it is, it sounds as if it's injured*, Kendra thought.

She had to tell Uncle Griffinskitch. Clutching her blanket around her, she raced out of her room, bare feet and all, and scampered up the stairs towards her uncle's room. Suddenly a strange shape, all hairy, hunched, and with a sunken face appeared from around the bend of the staircase. Kendra shrieked in surprise as a bony hand reached out to hold her tight.

"Don't play the fool! It's me, Uncle Griffinskitch."

Kendra opened her eyes and was greeted with the familiar face of her uncle. It was no wonder he had frightened her, for he was a ghostly figure at the best of times, never mind in the dark, with some strange thing wandering around outside. He had sharp blue eyes and a crooked nose, and his bent body leaned heavily upon the support of the short staff that he always carried in his thin and gnarled hands. Perhaps the most striking thing about Uncle Griffinskitch was his beard, for it was long and white, and covered his entire body, right down to his toes. But Kendra was relieved to see her uncle. He was a strong old man, and a gifted wizard too; some said the best in all the land. And wizardry was something they just might need this harrowing night.

"Are you all right?" Uncle Griffinskitch asked.

"Yes—you startled me, that's all," Kendra replied.

"Didn't mean to," he told her softly. "But keep your voice—"

"There's something out there," she interrupted. "And it's not Een."

He gave her a nod that told her that he had heard it too. They sat there for a moment in the dark, listening. The night, so wild and stormy, suddenly seemed peculiarly quiet.

But the silence was brief. After a moment, a loud, alarming knock cut through the darkness. Whatever *it* was, it was now banging on their door.

"Humph," Uncle Griffinskitch muttered. "We have company."

He lifted his staff and waved his hand over it so that its round top began to glow faintly.

"What are you going to do?" Kendra whispered.

"Answer the door of course," the old Een said, illuminating the stairs with his staff as though it were a torch. "I suppose there's no use in asking you to stay up here."

Kendra opened her mouth to protest, but her uncle cut her off. "Of course not."

The knock came again, loud and threatening.

5

Uncle Griffinskitch grunted and hobbled down the winding staircase, Kendra close behind him.

"HURRY!" bellowed a deep voice from outside.

The voice sent a shiver down Kendra's braids, but her Uncle only grumbled a sharp "Humph." His annoyed tone made Kendra feel better; it meant the old wizard wasn't frightened. Most Eens, of course, would be terrified at even the *thought* of a knock in the middle of a stormy night. But not Uncle Griffinskitch. Nothing seemed to ruffle him.

Uncle Griffinskitch now unlatched the door, and as it swung inward, Kendra screamed in spite of herself. For the thing that hulked in their doorway was definitely no Een. And it was bigger than a badger, too—much bigger.

"Kandlestar," the creature grunted.

It was too large to enter the house, but it plunged its giant cavernous face forward just the same, directly into the light of Uncle Griffinskitch's staff.

"An Unger!" Kendra cried. "You're an Unger! Uncle Griffinskitch—how? It's impossible for any monster—er, creature—er, anything other than an Een, to get through the magic curtain!"

"Yes, I know—hush," her uncle scolded.

"Kandlestar," the giant gasped again.

Kendra knew Ungers all too well. She had once saved one from death, out there in the wilds that lay beyond the magic curtain that protected the Eens from the outside world. That creature had just been a youngster, and she had been able to find the courage to help him. But now—this was completely different, for here was a fully-grown Unger standing in their doorway, right here in the land of Een—where they were supposed to be safe from such creatures.

6

Timidly, Kendra peered from behind the open door and studied the beast. The Unger was gargantuan. He looked as if he had been hewn from stone, for his skin was gray and hard, knotted with wrinkles and blemishes. Two giant tusks jutted

out from the corners of his mouth. He was very old, Kendra could tell, for his hair was ghost white and his skin paper-thin. But there was something more—a streak of blood was running down the Unger's face.

"He's wounded!" Kendra exclaimed, reaching towards the mighty Unger.

"NO, CHILD!" Uncle Griffinskitch ordered, pulling her back with a surprisingly strong hand.

The Unger pointed a crooked claw at Kendra. "Childs of Kandlestar," it moaned. "Youzum. Unger seekzum youzum."

"How do you know who I am?" Kendra asked.

"Quiet, I say!" Uncle Griffinskitch cried, casting a critical glare in her direction. He turned back and stared directly into the creature's giant, round eyes. "She's not the one you seek."

"Itzum her," the Unger groaned. He shot out a claw and grabbed Kendra's arm. He twisted her wrist so that her hand was visible in the light of Uncle Griffinskitch's staff. The Unger's grip was tight—but also remarkably gentle. "Eeneez marked withzum star."

Kendra stared down at her palm. She could see nothing—just the normal lines that had always run across her hand.

But the Unger seemed to see something more. "Unger can seezum mark," the mighty creature said, releasing Kendra's wrist. "Youzum Kandlestar . . . youzum key. Unger prophecy sayzum Een withzum star must gozum to Greeven Wastes by first summerzum moon."

"The Greeven Wastes?" Uncle Griffinskitch asked. "Where is that?"

"And why should I go there?" Kendra added.

"There youzum finds Door to Unger."

Kendra looked at her uncle for some sign that he knew what the creature was speaking of—but the old man only shook his head in confusion.

"Timezee runszum short," the Unger said gravely. "Door openzum but oncezum year—nightzum of first summerzum moon. Youzum findz it before then, Kandlestar! Otherwize it too latezum!"

"Humph," Uncle Griffinskitch muttered, banging his staff loudly against the floor. "None of this makes sense. Now see here—"

"Oroook," the Unger interrupted. "Unger's namezum Oroook. Eeneez mustzum trust Oroook. Oroook knewzum motherzum of Kandlestar."

"My mother!" Kendra gasped. "Where is she?"

"You're talking nonsense!" Uncle Griffinskitch told the Unger. "Kayla Kandlestar would never befriend a—"

"Oroook speakzum truth!" the Unger interjected again. "But now Oroook havezum no time lefts. Oroook wounded . . . listenzum! Youzum, Kandlestar, youzum must findzum Door to Unger."

"Why?" Uncle Griffinskitch demanded.

"Itzum doorzum to truths," the Unger groaned, falling to his knees in pain. "Truthzum about Eens! Truthzum . . . about family of Kandlestar! Een child must findzum Door to Unger. Rememberzum, by first summerzum moon!"

He grunted and his final breath was sharp and edged with a whistling sound. Then he closed his large eyes and slumped forward against their house, so hard that they could feel the tree bend against his great weight. He was so big that he completely blocked the doorway.

"Days of Een!" Uncle Griffinskitch uttered. "He's dead!"

And then, before their very eyes, the fallen creature faded away and disappeared. There was no puff of smoke, no sudden flash—he just melted into the darkness and was gone.

Kendra rubbed her eyes. *I'm still dreaming*, she thought. *I must be. This still must be a dream.*

Quickly, Uncle Griffinskitch closed the door. He shuffled to the kitchen table, only a few paces away, and fell heavily into his chair. He looked at Kendra with a strange expression on his face.

"It didn't really happen," she announced, somehow hoping that her uncle would agree with her.

But he didn't. And, in fact, the next day when the rain clouds scattered before the sun, Kendra discovered that it *had* to have happened. For there, pressed into the thick black mud before their doorway, was a set of enormous three-toed prints—the type of footprints that could only belong to an Unger.

CHAPTER 2

The Story of How Uncle Griffinskitch Found Kendra

Kendra was bursting with questions. "I don't understand," she said to her uncle at breakfast. "How did Oroook get into Een? Was it magic? How does he know my mother? Does that mean she's still alive? And what does any of it have to do with this Door to Unger?"

"Humph," Uncle Griffinskitch replied, sipping on his dandelion tea. Kendra knew the old wizard well enough to know that his humph meant he was in deep thought and that he didn't feel like talking. Indeed, his only words came after breakfast, when he said, "Go out to the garden today, Kendra, and rake over the Unger's footprints. If anyone finds them, there will be panic across Een."

Kendra nodded and watched her uncle disappear up the staircase. She knew she would not see him for the rest of the day. He would shut himself away in his chambers at the top of the cottage, studying his ancient manuscripts and other magical items.

The house in which Kendra and Uncle Griffinskitch lived had been built around the trunk of an old yew tree. Because of this, the floor plan was very much the shape of a donut—you could see the trunk no matter where you were standing in the cottage. Also, from the bottom floor, you could see straight up to the ceiling because of how the staircase wound around the trunk, shooting off here and there to reach different rooms. Still, despite the fact that the cottage was so small and open, Kendra was rarely able to sneak into Uncle Griffinskitch's private chambers. He kept them hidden with passwords and secret doorways, mostly to keep Kendra out, for the old wizard was ever-weary of her curious nature.

With her uncle gone, Kendra set about cleaning up the garden. The sun was shining warmly now and, to Kendra, the stormy night, with its mysterious events, seemed as if it had happened long ago. Of course, the footprints in the mud were enough to remind her just how real the Unger had been.

"The strange thing about these tracks is that they don't come from anywhere," Kendra said to herself. "They just start right here by the garden shed."

The fortunate thing about this was that it was easy to remove any trace of the Unger. After an hour's work, Kendra was confident that no one would ever know that the creature had been there.

Uncle Griffinskitch did not emerge from his chambers until late that night, but when he finally did, his eyes were red and tired.

"Did you discover anything?" Kendra asked him eagerly.

"Humph," he muttered irritably. "I could not find any mention of this 'Door to Unger' in my books or parchments."

"But we have to find the door," Kendra said. "The Unger said it would help me find my family."

"Humph," Uncle Griffinskitch said again. He sat down in his favorite chair, next to the kitchen fireplace. Kendra had started a fire to cook dinner, and the room glowed with warm orange light. The old Een stroked his beard and stared uncomfortably at Kendra.

"What is it?" she asked, tugging on her braids nervously.

"It's your family," Uncle Griffinskitch replied after a moment. "There's something I've never told you about how they disappeared."

"What do you mean?" Kendra asked. "Why haven't you told me?"

"I wanted to wait until you were twelve," Uncle Griffinskitch explained. "As you know, twelve is an important age for Eens. It's the age you finish school. It's the age you can begin an apprenticeship with a master. It's when you're old enough to understand certain things."

"I can understand now," Kendra declared. "I'm almost twelve anyhow."

"But this isn't about them," the old wizard said.

"But I thought you said—,"

"It's about *you*," Uncle Griffinskitch murmured, leaning forward in his chair. "You see, long ago, when you were just a baby, your mother and the rest of your family disappeared."

"I know," Kendra said, sitting at her uncle's feet. "They were traveling in the outside world, beyond the magic curtain."

"Aye," Uncle Griffinskitch said. "But what you don't know is that *you* were with them."

"What?!" Kendra exclaimed. "Then how come I didn't disappear with them?"

"I don't know," the old wizard admitted, his wrinkled face flickering in the light of the fire. "I went after your family with hopes of bringing them back. But I didn't find them. I only found you, wrapped in your tiny green blanket, lying on the rocks. Everywhere, there were Unger footprints. But you were safe."

"Ungers took my family?" Kendra asked.

"It seemed that way," Uncle Griffinskitch said. "But the thing is, they didn't take *you*."

"Maybe they couldn't find me," Kendra suggested.

"No, I think they did find you," Uncle Griffinskitch said. "They just didn't take you. They left you behind."

"But why?" Kendra asked.

"I have often wondered," Uncle Griffinskitch said, leaning back in his chair with a sigh. "There's some connection between you and the Ungers, Kendra. They left you behind as a baby. Then last year, you saved one. And then . . . there was last night."

"Why would the Ungers take my family?" Kendra asked.

"Because they detest Eens," Uncle Griffinskitch said solemnly. "That's why."

"That Unger I saved last year—Trooogul—he said he didn't hate us," Kendra said. "He said it was the Eens that hate the Ungers."

"Then he was lying!" Uncle Griffinskitch cried, his face flushing red. "The only reason he said that is because you had just saved his sorry hide! Of course the Ungers hate us! That's why they took your family! That's why they set out to destroy all of Een!"

Kendra lifted her hand and stared at her palm. "But Trooogul didn't hurt me," she murmured once her uncle's ire seemed to fade. "And the Ungers left me behind as a baby. Is it because of this mark, Uncle Griffinskitch? This mark that the Unger Oroook saw upon my palm?"

"It may be so," Uncle Griffinskitch muttered.

"I wish Oroook had told us more," Kendra said. "I still don't know how he was able to cross the magic curtain. Only Eens and Een animals should be able to go in and out of Een. Oroook should have never even found the curtain or the land of Een—it should be invisible to him."

"And yet his tracks didn't come from the curtain," Uncle Griffinskitch mused, stroking his whiskery chin. "I examined them myself, before sunrise."

"You're right," Kendra agreed. "The footprints only started in our garden. It's as if the Unger just magically appeared."

"This whole thing is a mystery," Uncle Griffinskitch said.

"What are we going to do?" Kendra asked.

"We shall pay a visit to Winter Woodsong tomorrow," Uncle Griffinskitch declared. "We are in grave need of her wisdom."

Kendra had met Winter Woodsong only twice. Even though she was very old, she was a powerful sorceress and the leader of the Council of Elders. Uncle Griffinskitch himself had once been an Elder of Een, but he had retired from the council after arguing with the other members—especially Burdock Brown.

"Elder Woodsong has been very ill," Kendra said. "Do you think she will be well enough to see us?"

"I hope so," Uncle Griffinskitch replied. "She may be the only one to help us find this mysterious Door to Unger."

CHAPTER 3

The Guardian at the Gate

Everyone needs to ask for help sometimes— even wizards. For this very reason, Uncle Griffinskitch awoke Kendra early the next morning, and they set off to make the short journey into the town of Faun's End. It was in Faun's End where they would find the Elder Stone, the magnificent palace where the Elders of Een held their private councils. More importantly, it was also the place where they would find the sorceress Winter Woodsong.

Kendra and her uncle made their way through the forest slowly, stopping here and there to pick a few flowers for old Winter Woodsong. They had only gone a short way when a small gray mouse came scampering from around a corner in the path and blundered right into Uncle Griffinskitch. The whiskered wizard tumbled to the ground in a fluff of white hair.

"Humph!" Uncle Griffinskitch grumbled, pulling himself up. "Who's this now?"

"Oki!" Kendra cried, for this was none other than her best friend. "Why are you in such a hurry?"

"Oh, hi, Kendra!" Oki squeaked. The little mouse was quite excitable by nature and he was now hopping impatiently from foot to foot. "I was just on my way to find your uncle."

"Consider him found," Uncle Griffinskitch grunted as he tried to brush some of the dirt out of his beard. "But why do you only ever find me by charging into me?"

"I'm sorry, Mr. Griffinskitch," Oki apologized. "But I have some terrible news!"

"Uh-oh," Kendra said. "This is how our adventures always begin, Oki. You bump into Uncle Griffinskitch and bring bad news."

"It's not my fault," Oki said. "I'm a messenger, after all. It's my job to deliver news. I can't help it if it's bad."

"Indeed," Uncle Griffinskitch said, furrowing his brow. "Well, what is it, young Oki?'

"It's Elder Woodsong, sir," the mouse replied. "She's taken a turn for the worse. She's become so ill that she can hardly get out of bed, and she's finally let Burdock bully her into retiring from the Council of Elders!"

"Humph," Uncle Griffinskitch grumbled, looking sharply at Oki. "Elder Woodsong has led the council for a hundred seasons! Who does Burdock think he is? Who will lead in Elder Woodsong's place?"

"Burdock himself, sir," Oki said with a gulp. "He's declared himself leader of the council."

"Days of Een!" Uncle Griffinskitch cried. "That's treacherous news for us all. When did this all happen?"

"Just this morning, sir," Oki explained.

"We were just on our way to see her," Kendra declared. "We have our own news."

"Oh, dear," Oki murmured. "What now?"

"We'll tell you later," Uncle Griffinskitch said to the tiny mouse. "For now, we must make haste to see Elder Woodsong."

They hurried on their way and soon arrived at Faun's End. The whole town was abuzz with the news that the mean-spirited Burdock Brown was now leading the Council of Elders. When the townspeople saw Uncle Griffinskitch they immediately crowded around and assailed him with questions.

"Have you heard about Elder Brown, Mr. Griffinskitch?"

"What will you do? Will you join the council again?"

"How can he do this to Elder Woodsong? Do you think she will recover?"

"Humph!" the old Een snorted at Kendra and Oki. "Let's get out of here as quickly as possible!"

They pushed their way through the crowd and crossed the bridge to the Elder Stone. Now for those of you who have never heard of the Elder Stone, let me tell you that it is a wondrous place. At first glance, you might have thought that the Elder Stone was just a plain old rock. But then, upon looking more closely, you would see that it was something quite marvelous.

For the Elder Stone was much like a castle, with rooms and passageways, doors and windows, and even a round moat. The outside of the stone was carved with hundreds of tiny pictures: stars and moons, or strange Een faces. Some of these faces had long, open mouths from which gushed sparkling waterfalls. The falls glistened in the sunlight, changing color as they tumbled from ledge to ledge and down to the moat below.

Kendra had always loved the sight of the beautiful Elder Stone, but there was no time to admire it now. They quickly approached the main door of the stone and knocked loudly.

After a moment, they were met by none other than Burdock Brown himself. The old Een was hunched and fat, and he seemed in possession of a permanent snarl. His eyes were dark and hard, and he had only one eyebrow; this was thick and black, and stretched across his forehead like a caterpillar.

Kendra, Oki, and Uncle Griffinskitch exchanged looks of surprise. Normally, the Elder Stone was guarded by Captain Jinx, a tiny grasshopper with legendary strength.

"What's going on here?" Kendra asked Burdock. "Where's Captain Jinx?"

"Jinx is no longer allowed here!" Burdock barked.

"Why?" Kendra asked. "What has she done?"

"Well, for starters, she was born a bug," Burdock retorted. "And there are no bugs allowed in the Elder Stone anymore. No animals either. No critters of any kind. Just Eens!"

"That is the most ridiculous thing I've ever heard!" Uncle Griffinskitch declared, banging his staff on the ground.

"No critters!" Oki squeaked. "But I'm a messenger for the Elders!"

"No longer," Burdock said, flashing a viperous smile. "I'm the head of the council now, and I have decided to put an end to all these animals running around the Elder Stone. These are dangerous times, after all. We can't be placing important Een matters in the hands—or, should I say, the paws and claws—of these critters."

"That's not fair!" Kendra cried. "Animals and Eens have lived together in peace and harmony for as long as . . . for as long as. . . . "

"As long as Een has existed," Uncle Griffinskitch finished, and Kendra could see his ears burning red with anger.

"Change is afoot, old one," Burdock said. "As I said, dangerous times."

"Humph," Uncle Griffinskitch muttered. "And what is so dangerous?"

"Surely, you know better than anyone, old one," Burdock said, his eyebrow twisting into a knot as he spoke. "Didn't you hear the strange noises two nights ago?"

Kendra gulped and cast a quick glance at her uncle. "Noise? What noises?" the old wizard asked, his voice steady and calm.

"Fine, be that way then," Burdock retorted. "But you and your troublesome little niece are no longer welcome at the Elder Stone."

"We're here to see Elder Woodsong," Uncle Griffinskitch declared. "She still keeps her chambers here, does she not? Or have you cast her out on the street?"

"Of course not," Burdock growled irritably.

"Then you can hardly deny me the company of my old friend," Uncle Griffinskitch declared, glaring sternly at Burdock. "Now get out of our way."

But Burdock didn't budge.

"Humph," Uncle Griffinskitch muttered. "Of course, if you prefer, I could change you into a mushroom, Burdock. Do you really want to engage in a wizard's duel this early in the day?"

"Go then," Burdock scowled, standing back. "But just you and the girl. No mice allowed! Check the laws—the Elders passed it just this past hour."

"I'm sure they did," Uncle Griffinskitch sneered. "You and your old cronies now! You've driven every other respectable Een off the council!"

"Uncle Griffinskitch, you can't let them keep Oki out!" Kendra cried.

"Now, now, it's okay," the old wizard said. He turned to Oki, and Kendra could hear him whisper these instructions to the tiny mouse: "Go, honest one. Gather our friends. You know who, right?"

Oki nodded. "Yes, sir, I know."

"Good," Uncle Griffinskitch said, patting Oki on his whiskery head. "Have them meet at my house, moon-up. And that includes you."

"I'll do it," Oki said, and he turned and darted across the bridge, back into the town of Faun's End.

"What's all the whispering about?" Burdock demanded.

"Never you mind," Uncle Griffinskitch told him with a glare. "You're not the king, Burdock. Not yet, anyway."

"Go on then," Burdock said. "I don't have the time to waste on rebellious folk like you, anyway. I have another important council meeting to attend."

"Indeed," Uncle Griffinskitch muttered and, with that, he lifted his head high and marched into the Elder Stone with

Kendra right at his heels, doing the best to emulate his stern attitude. Together they brushed past Burdock Brown and began the long climb up the Elder Stone towards the private chambers of the ancient Een sorceress, Winter Woodsong.

CHAPTER 4

A Visit to Winter Woodsong

Kendra

could see that her uncle was quite out of breath by the time they reached the top of the Elder Stone. However, he did not even pause to collect himself before rapping on the small wooden door that belonged to Winter Woodsong.

After a moment, they were greeted by a weak, quiet voice that said, "Enter, old friend."

Kendra cast a startled look at her uncle. How could Elder Woodsong know who they were? But the old wizard merely grunted and opened the door to enter a small, round room.

Kendra cast her eyes around the chamber in awe. If her own house was a

25

collection of odd furniture and strange items (she lived with a wizard, after all), then Elder Woodsong's home was even more so. Everywhere she looked, there was something interesting to see: kettles and cauldrons, goblets and caskets, wooden chests under lock and key, and tattered parchments and papers. In one corner of the room, there stood a tall cuckoo clock, which chimed almost immediately upon their arrival. Much to Kendra's delight, the clock featured not a cuckoo, but a small wooden Goojun that banged a tiny toy club as he traveled his short mechanical path. In another corner, there was a large metallic globe with long rods jutting out at different angles. Each rod was capped with a small glowing light, and it seemed to Kendra that the strange device was somehow a map of the stars and planets. There were also many books scattered about the chamber. Many of these were stacked in tall piles, while others were lying open to reveal strange figures and symbols that Kendra could not begin to decipher.

Then her gaze fell upon the old sorceress herself. Winter was lying on a small cot in the corner of the room, the blankets pulled tight about her frail body. Her hair was white and tangled, and wrinkles crisscrossed her pale, drawn face.

"Elder Woodsong," Uncle Griffinskitch said, immediately going to her. "How fare you?"

"I'm stronger than some would say," Winter said. She tried to sit up in her bed, but immediately broke into a sharp, hacking cough.

"Now, now," Uncle Griffinskitch said, gently taking her hand. "Just rest. We shan't stay long."

"Oh, no need to leave so quickly," Winter said. "The company is welcome."

"We brought you some flowers, Elder Woodsong," Kendra said.

"Ah, thank you," the old woman said, taking the bouquet and placing them in a vase by her bed. "Fireflowers are my favorite; their fragrance is divine. Did you know they grow only here, in the land of Een?"

"No," Kendra said shyly, suddenly timid in the presence of the great sorceress.

"Well, no matter," Winter said. "Take a seat, child. Sit, sit."

There was hardly a chair to be found, for each seemed to be stacked with books. After giving her braids a nervous tug, Kendra discovered a small empty stool near Winter's bed. She was now met with some surprise, however; for as soon as she seated herself, the stool seemed to shoot up, so that Kendra found herself sitting high up in the air.

"It's a bothersome seat, that one," Winter remarked with some amusement. "It has a mind of its own."

"Oh!" Kendra exclaimed, her feet dangling in the air.

"Down, seat, down!" Winter ordered, and the stool instantly returned to its former height. "Sorry, child," Winter murmured. "I suppose such are the hazards of visiting a sorceress!"

Uncle Griffinskitch glared at Kendra (as if *she* were somehow responsible for the mischievous seat) then turned to Winter and said, "What's this I hear about Burdock forcing you to step down?"

"Burdock hungers for power," Winter sighed. "That much is clear to me now. He would be emperor, I think, if Eens were to tolerate such nonsense."

"Humph," Uncle Griffinskitch muttered. "I won't let Burdock get away with this."

"Shun your anger, old friend," Winter said. "Burdock has already achieved his purpose. Myself, I am too old now to oppose him."

"He has declared it illegal for animals to enter the Elder Stone," Uncle Griffinskitch declared. "He's fired Captain Jinx and Honest Oki."

Winter sighed and closed her eyes, and to Kendra, it appeared as if she looked incredibly tired. "This is most unfortunate," Winter murmured after a moment. "Burdock's heart has grown dark."

"I'm going to take you home with me," Uncle Griffinskitch announced. "Kendra and I will tend to you."

"No," Winter said, opening her eyes wide at the wizard. "This is my home, and I shall stay here. Do I seem so weak to your young eyes?"

Kendra smiled in spite of herself; she had never known anyone to refer to her uncle as young.

"Besides, you don't look so well yourself," Winter told the wizard. "Why, you look as if you've seen a ghost."

"I just may have," Uncle Griffinskitch muttered gravely.

"Hmmm?" Winter asked, pushing herself up in her bed.

Uncle Griffinskitch stroked his long white beard and began to tell the old sorceress about the visit from the Unger. He went through the story slowly, careful to not leave out any details.

Winter Woodsong listened patiently. "This is most curious, most curious indeed," she murmured when he was done.

"Have you ever heard of this Door to Unger?" Uncle Griffinskitch asked.

"No," Winter replied. "I have seen no reference to it in any of the ancient texts. As far as I know, there is no land of Unger. So how could there be a door to it?"

"My thoughts exactly," Uncle Griffinskitch said. "Perhaps it's just a fable."

"Perhaps," Winter said. "But I don't think so. Many things lie out there, beyond the magic curtain, of which we Eens are ignorant. And, from what you say, this Unger gave his life to tell you of the door."

Kendra had managed to keep quiet up to this point, but now her anxiety got the better of her. "But how could an Unger get through the magic curtain?" she blurted.

"Some strange magic, for sure," Winter said. "But I do not think he truly crossed the curtain. I think he transported himself to the exact spot outside of your house. Then, just as he died, he transported himself away. He must have been a wizard."

"An Unger wizard?" Uncle Griffinskitch scoffed. "I have never head of such a thing."

"And you have heard of everything, have you?" Winter scolded, but the effort of raising her voice caused her to break into a fitful cough again.

Kendra turned red with embarrassment for her uncle; very few dared to speak to him in such a manner.

"Of course, we have another clue," Winter said. "You say the Unger mentioned a place called the Greeven Wastes?"

"Aye," Uncle Griffinskitch said. "I suppose you think this has something to do with the Wizard Greeve?"

"Don't you?" Winter asked.

"Humph," Uncle Griffinskitch muttered; and it was a peculiar humph, one Kendra couldn't quite decipher.

"Who's the Wizard Greeve?" Kendra asked.

"He was a first Elder of Een," Winter replied gravely. "Here, pass me that book, child, and I will show you the tale."

CHAPTER 5

The Legend of the Wizard Greeve

There were many books scattered about, but Kendra immediately guessed the one Winter wanted, for it was old and tattered, and had a mysterious quality about it. She passed it to the sorceress.

"Few know of the legend," Winter explained, opening the book on her lap. "The Elders don't really like to speak of it. Indeed, there's only one other copy of this book; your uncle has that one. Now where's the place . . . ah, yes. Here it is. Read this, child."

She handed the book back to Kendra, just as her stool sprouted upwards again.

"Down seat, down I say!" Winter cried.

With this admonishment, the stool slowly lowered; Kendra could have sworn that she heard it sigh.

"I'll really have to get that fixed," Winter said apologetically. "But that's for another day. Read the legend, Kendra. It starts at the top of page 251."

Kendra wriggled firm in her seat (to brace herself against any further mischief on the stool's part) and then read the following words:

In the Days of Een, when all were one, goodness flourished in the lands and the race of Eens knew only happiness. In those ancient times, there came to be the first council of Elders. Upon seven seats in the Elder Stone sat seven Elders, and they were all brothers. For many seasons, these first Elders guided the Eens wisely; but one brother, the Wizard Greeve, came to know envy and hatred. He desired to lord power over his brethren and so he used his dark arts to plot against them.

But one of the brothers, the Elder Longbraids, discovered the treachery of the Wizard Greeve. And so it came to pass that six brothers turned against one; and they banished Greeve from the lands of Een.

To the north did the dark wizard journey, to the verdant plains, rushing rivers, and lush forests did he carry his wickedness. And there did he construct a temple, a deep underground maze that served as a terrible monument to his fiendish heart; and in that place the plants withered, the rivers shrank, and the great trees fell. That place became a wasteland and there, in that jumble of rock and ruin, did the heart of the Wizard Greeve swell with hunger for revenge against his brothers.

And so it came to pass that the Wizard Greeve devised a plot to triumph over the remaining Elders of Een. Each of them did he vanquish with his dark arts, each of them knew his dark heart—save for one. The lone survivor, the Elder Longbraids, fled

to Een, his beloved land, his heart afflicted by his brother's deed. And now did Elder Longbraids seal off the land of Een by the spell of the magic curtain, a great barrier he did create so that the land might be protected from the hideous monsters that came to skitter or crawl or slither across the wide earth. The Wizard Greeve, his heart was not soothed after exacting revenge upon his brothers. His hatred remains yet, in that wretched place, and all who trespass there come to know the curse of Greeve . . .

As she finished, Kendra gave her braids a long tug, thinking deeply. "So this place—where the Wizard Greeve went to live—this could be the same place that the Unger called the Greeven Wastes," she said presently.

"It would appear so," Winter said.

"I still don't know what all of this has to do with the Door to Unger," Kendra mused.

"As the legend says, the Wizard Greeve constructed a maze in the wastelands," Winter explained. "Perhaps the door leads to the maze. All we seem to know from your Unger visitor is that the door is located in the Greeven Wastes and that it opens but once a year."

"But there's something strange about this legend," Kendra remarked. "It seems as if something's missing."

"Aye," Uncle Griffinskitch muttered rather testily. "There are some who believe there is more to the legend, that part of it has been lost through the ages."

"Do we know what became of the Wizard Greeve?" Kendra asked. "Do we know what his curse is?"

Winter smiled weakly at her then turned to Uncle Griffinskitch. "Old friend," she said, "do me a favor and go to my study. You'll find a book there called *Spells of the Ancients*. I would look at it."

Uncle Griffinskitch nodded and said, "Come, Kendra."

"No, let the child stay with me," Winter said.

"Humph," Uncle Griffinskitch mumbled, which Kendra knew was his way of saying, "Very well."

"No one knows the nature of Greeve's curse," Winter told Kendra once the old man had left. "But I can tell you one thing, child: the curse was something that was of great interest to your mother."

"Really?" Kendra asked excitedly. "Why?"

"She felt the Legend of Greeve was somehow important to Eens, here and now in the present," Winter explained. "But her interest upset the Elders, even her brother—your Uncle Griffinskitch. The two argued about it endlessly. Your uncle called her interest in the legend an obsession." The old sorceress paused for a moment. Then she said, "It's my belief,

Kendra, that your mother left Een to try and find the Greeven Wastes, all those years ago."

"Oroook said he knew my mother," Kendra said.

"Perhaps he did," Winter said. "If the Ungers took your family, then Oroook certainly had the chance to meet her. I can tell you this, child: if you go in search of the Door to Unger, you may well be following in the footsteps of your family."

"Then I must go in search of it," Kendra said. "Don't you think, Elder Woodsong?"

A faint smile played across Winter's face again and she closed her eyes, as if deep in thought. For several minutes she said nothing, and Kendra sat in silent discomfort, wondering whether the old woman had fallen asleep. After what seemed like an eternity to Kendra, Winter raised one of her frail hands and pointed to a large panel of artwork that was carved into the stone wall right above her tiny bed. The carving looked very old. It had once been painted, but most of the color had chipped or faded away.

"An interesting picture, isn't it?" Winter asked, looking at Kendra. "Tell me, child, what do you see?"

Kendra had no idea what the scene had to do with the Wizard Greeve, or with finding her mother. But that seemed Winter's way, to always speak in riddles, so Kendra turned her attention to the stone carving. In it she could see tiny Een people (she could tell them by their braided hair) mixed in between giant monsters: there were Ungers, Goojuns, Izzards, Orrids, and Krakes. To Kendra, it looked like some of the figures were holding staffs, or maybe spears.

"I see monsters and Eens," Kendra replied after a moment. "It looks like there is a great battle between the two sides."

"Hmmm," Winter murmured mysteriously. "It is a most curious picture. Of all the carvings to be found on the Elder Stone—inside or out—this one is the oldest."

Just then Uncle Griffinskitch reappeared. "I could not find your book," the old wizard said. "Are you sure it was last in your study?"

"Oh, dear," Winter said, reaching beneath her pillow to reveal a small black book. "It would appear that I had it with me all along. Sorry to send you on such an errant mission, old friend. In any case, I suppose I don't need to look at the book at all now."

"Humph," Uncle Griffinskitch muttered and Kendra could not help to notice a mischievous twinkle in Winter's clear blue eyes.

"Kendra and I were just discussing the Door to Unger," the old sorceress said. "It seems to me that you should leave as soon as possible if you hope to find it before the first summer moon."

"And who has decided we are going?" Uncle Griffinskitch asked hotly.

"But we have to!" Kendra cried. "This could be our only chance to find our family, Uncle Griffinskitch."

"As far as we know, the Ungers could be trying to lure us into a trap," the old wizard grumbled.

"Anything is possible," Winter said. "But I think it's a chance you'll have to take. For many years, the disappearance of your family has been a mystery. Finally, a crack of light is showing through a door that has otherwise been closed. Follow that light, old friend, follow it."

Uncle Griffinskitch stroked his long beard, deep in thought. "Humph," he muttered after a moment. "On your advice, we shall go in search of this door. May the ancients help us in such a quest!"

They bid the old woman farewell and made their way down the stairways of the Elder Stone. Kendra's mind was racing. Everything was happening so quickly. Elder Woodsong was gravely ill, Burdock Brown had made himself leader of the council, and somehow they had to find a mysterious door in a fabled wasteland, which could be anywhere in the outside world. On top of that, they had only a few weeks in which to do it.

Things couldn't get much more complicated, Kendra thought to herself.

But, as she was to soon find out, she couldn't have been more wrong.

BY ORDER OF THE COUNCIL OF EEN ELDERS.

THE MAGIC CURTAIN HAS BEEN SEALED
BY MAGIC ENCHANTMENT
FOREVER.
THIS MEASURE HAS BEEN TAKEN
TO PROTECT THE LAND OF EEN
FROM THE OUTSIDE WORLD.

ANYONE WHO ATTEMPTS TO BREAK
THE MAGIC OF THE SEAL,
OR TRIES TO LEAVE THE LAND OF EEN,
WILL BE CONSIDERED A TRAITOR
AND WILL BE IMPRISONED IMMEDIATELY.

SIGNED, BURDOCK BROWN

CHAPTER 6

A M∞nlight Meeting

YOU have probably
been told that it's rude
to stare. If that's true,
then the town of
Faun's End was a
very rude place as
Kendra and her
uncle crossed the
bridge from the Elder
Stone and entered the
busy town square. Everyone
seemed to suddenly stop and look
at them.

"Humph," Uncle Griffinskitch
grunted. "What's going on here?"

"Oh, you won't like this!" said
Gilburt Green, the town baker.

"Eh? What's that?" the old
wizard asked.

Gilburt turned and pointed to a
large board that had been nailed to a
signpost in the center of the town square.
Kendra and her uncle quickly pushed their

way through the crowd and looked upon the sign. It had been freshly painted, and read:

By order of the Council of Een Elders

The magic curtain has been sealed
by magic enchantment
FOREVER.
This measure has been taken
to protect the Land of Een
from the outside world.
Anyone who attempts to break the magic of the seal,
or tries to leave the Land of Een, will be considered a traitor
and will be imprisoned immediately.

Signed, Burdock Brown

"Oh no!" Kendra gasped. "We'll never find my family now! We'll never find the Door to—"

"Hush now, Kendra," Uncle Griffinskitch said quickly, ushering her away from the crowd that was gathered around the sign. "Everywhere there are ears. We must be careful with our words. We can trust a precious few now."

"Everything has changed," Kendra whispered to her uncle as they headed back to their home. "Almost overnight."

"Humph," Uncle Griffinskitch grunted in agreement. "A tree will rot for fifty years—and then suddenly it falls."

Later that night, as the white moon gazed down upon the tiny land of Een, a secret meeting took place in the yew tree house where Kendra and her uncle lived. Six in all crowded around the candlelit table in the small kitchen. Joining Uncle Griffinskitch and Kendra were four important friends. The first of these, of course, was Honest Oki the mouse, who was Kendra's closest companion. Next was Juniper Jinx, the fiery grasshopper who just that morning had been fired from her job as the Captain of the Een guard. Jinx was the smallest creature at the table, but she was also the strongest, for as a young child she had accidentally swallowed a potion that had given her super strength. Next at the table was Professor Bumblebean, a tall and well-mannered Een who was the head of the famous Een Library in Faun's End. Professor Bumblebean was quite bookish in appearance, for he had a small pair of glasses perched precariously on the end of his large nose and he had a stubby pencil tucked behind his ear. Last, was Ratchet Ringtail, the outspoken raccoon who fancied himself an amateur wizard and extraordinary inventor. He was also known as somewhat of a troublemaker, but he was a close and loyal friend to Kendra.

Despite their differences in appearance and personality, everyone at the table had one thing in common: They had all journeyed together in the world outside of the magic curtain. Now Uncle Griffinskitch had a plan to lead them on another adventure, this time to find the mysterious Door to Unger.

As the candle burned down through the night, the old wizard told the company of the strange visit by the Unger, and of the creature's mysterious message. There were many gasps and looks of astonishment, but all were quiet as Uncle Griffinskitch spoke.

At last the old and whiskered Een finished by saying, "So, now you see my purpose in calling you all here this night. Ken-

dra and I are leaving Een to find this Door to Unger. Hopefully this will lead us to our family. And we need your help."

"I'm in," Ratchet said immediately. "I'll go with you, Kendra, wherever you would go."

"Thank you," Kendra said, feeling better just knowing that the large raccoon would be at her side.

"You can count on me too," Jinx said, raising her sword in salute to the mission. "I'd rather fight monsters along with you, Kendra, than end up in Burdock's dungeon—which is sure to happen if I stay here. It's taking all my will to stop myself from charging into the Elder Stone and sticking my swords, one by one, into Burdock like the fat pincushion that he is."

Kendra smiled in the candlelight. Good old Jinx; her tongue was sharper than her swords, but her courage and strength would be a welcome addition to their quest.

"I do say, you won't go on this journey without my company," Professor Bumblebean declared. "I suspect you will need my books and great learning, after all."

That left only Oki. Everyone turned to look at the small gray mouse. "There's nothing I can do," Oki squeaked. "Of course I'd like to come. But my parents will never let me leave Een again. Not after all the dangers we ran into last time."

"But Oki," Kendra spoke up. "You've already had your twelfth birthday."

"I don't see how that helps," Oki said.

"Once you're twelve you can apprentice with a master," Kendra explained. "And if you're master goes somewhere, then you *must* follow him."

"But I don't have a master," Oki said.

"I would certainly take you," Professor Bumblebean remarked. "However, I've been engaged in teaching our Captain Jinx—or should I say former Captain Jinx—now just Jinx, I suppose, in learning the art of letters."

Everyone just stared at the professor, for he loved to use such big words that few could ever understand him.

"I think what Professor Bumblebean is trying to say is that he is teaching Jinx how to read," Oki said after a moment.

"Of course that's what I said," Professor Bumblebean remarked. "I do say, how could I have been much clearer? Our poor Jinx never learned properly how to read, so I have taken it upon myself to instruct her."

"All right, that's enough," Jinx said shyly. "I don't know how I manage to spend so many hours with you at once, *Bumblebore.*"

"My word," Professor Bumblebean said, pushing his glasses up the bridge of his nose. "I thought we discussed, dear Jinx, that you would no longer make fun of my name."

"Sorry," Jinx said with a shrug. "Old habits die hard."

"The point is, we need a master for Oki," Kendra said.

"Well, heck, I've always wanted a slave," Ratchet declared. "I'll take Oki."

"No, not a slave, Ratchet," Kendra told him. "An apprentice. You have to teach him things."

"Oh, of course," Ratchet said.

"Well, what are you going to teach him?" Uncle Griffinskitch asked.

"Inventing of course," Ratchet said indignantly, with a slight scowl on his masked face.

"Oh dear," Oki murmured.

"Look, do you want to come with us or not?" Ratchet said. "And besides, who wouldn't want to learn from me? I'm a wizard of sorts, after all, and an inventor of—"

"Yes, yes, we know," Uncle Griffinskitch interrupted. "An inventor of extraordinary talent and magical inspiration."

"Exactly," Ratchet said.

"Well, it's settled then," Professor Bumblebean declared cheerfully. "We're all agreed to form a company to go out and find this Door to Unger!"

"Er . . . Uncle Griffinskitch, there's just one problem," Kendra said, tugging her braids nervously. "If the curtain is sealed, how are we going to actually leave Een?"

"It's a grave problem," Uncle Griffinskitch admitted, leaning back in his chair and stroking his long whiskers. "But I am hoping that I can rupture the enchanted seal with my own magic."

"But if you're caught, Burdock will imprison you," Kendra warned.

"It's a chance I'll have to take," the old wizard said.

"You know, there just might be another possibility," Professor Bumblebean declared. "You all know, of course, of the statue called the *Fallen Faun*, which stands near the Een Library? Well, beneath the statue is an ancient crypt."

"What's a crypt?" Ratchet asked.

"An underground burial chamber," Professor Bumblebean explained. "It's here where Flavius Faun was laid to rest. Flavius, as you know, was the creature that Faun's End was named for. I have given tours of this crypt. It's very grand, and has many statues and artifacts—,"

"To the point, professor," Uncle Griffinskitch said.

"Well," the professor continued, as if he hadn't even noticed the interruption, "legend has it that somewhere within the crypt is a secret tunnel that leads to the outside world."

"I've never heard of this legend," Jinx said.

"Humph . . . neither have I," Uncle Griffinskitch said. "But, as a friend recently pointed out to me, I don't know everything. How do you know of this legend, professor?"

"Why, I read about it of course," Professor Bumblebean replied happily.

"Do you think this tunnel really exists, professor?" Kendra asked eagerly.

"Certainly," Professor Bumblebean said. "We'll have to make a thorough search of the crypt, of course. The story says that the door to this tunnel is well concealed."

"What does that mean?" Ratchet asked.

"It means, dear friends," said the professor, "that you just won't find it sitting beneath your nose."

CHAPTER 7

Ratchet Ringtail Has an Explosive Idea

Throughout

history, there have been many explorers and famous adventurers who have searched for fabled treasures and secret vaults. Many of them have spent entire lifetimes in pursuit of such hidden mysteries. The problem for Kendra and her friends was that they didn't have an entire lifetime to spend searching. Somehow they had to find the secret tunnel out of Een—and they had to do it quickly. Kendra knew that if they couldn't discover a way to the outside world soon, they would never find the Door to Unger before the first summer's moon. And that meant they might *never* find her family.

So, while Uncle Griffinskitch attempted to crack through the curtain with his magic, Kendra and her friends spent each day searching the crypt that lay beneath the large stone statue, the *Fallen Faun*. The crypt was normally not open to the public without permission, but in this matter they were lucky, for Professor Bumblebean had his own key. He was, after all, the local expert on the history of Faun's End, and he often led visitors on tours of the mysterious underground chamber.

Kendra found the crypt itself to be a rather exciting place. There was a small door at the base of the statue, which, when opened, revealed a long staircase that was so dark and dank that it was impossible to descend without the aid of a torch. The chamber at the end of the stairs was even blacker. The floor was paved with square stones that were marked with strange symbols, and the walls were comprised of mostly rock and dirt, giving the whole place the same eerie feeling that a cave might have. As Professor Bumblebean had first described, it was cluttered with many statues and strange objects from days long ago. Of course, the centerpiece of the crypt was the long casket that held the bones of Flavius Faun. The casket was quite ornate, and it was carved with a very life-like relief of the legendary creature.

Day after day, Kendra and her friends searched for the secret tunnel that might allow them escape into the outside world. A week passed, and they had still found no trace of the tunnel.

"I wonder if this secret passageway even exists," Kendra said as she, Oki, and Ratchet walked home one evening after a particularly long day of searching.

"Well, you can't expect to find it under your nose, as Bumblebean would say," Ratchet declared.

Kendra managed a laugh, for the professor had indeed become very fond of saying that very thing at the start of each day.

"Well, I loathe that crypt," Oki declared. "It's so dark and gloomy. Plus, I don't like the idea of thinking that Flavius Faun is buried down there."

"He won't hurt you," Ratchet said. "He's just a pile of bones now."

"The point is, I'm already terrified, and the adventure hasn't even begun yet," Oki said.

"Just use your onion trick," Ratchet told him. "Remember, you used to always try to *not* think of onions, and then you'd be so distracted that you'd forget you were scared."

"Not anymore," Oki informed the raccoon. "I used to think of onions (or try *not* to think of them), but then I met that plant on our last adventure that turned me into an onion because it could read my mind. So now I try to not think of turnips."

"That doesn't make any sense, Oki," Kendra told her whiskery little friend. "If you were to meet that same plant, he would just turn you into a turnip instead of an onion."

"True," Oki said. "But one of Professor Bumblebean's books said that onions are the favorite food of Izzards. So I'd much rather be turned into a turnip. I don't think *anyone* would want to eat a turnip. Not even an Izzard."

"The mouse has a point," Ratchet said. "You know, you will make a good slave, Oki."

"No, not a slave, Ratchet!" Kendra scolded. "An *apprentice*."

"Yeah, that's what I meant," Ratchet said. "Sorry, we inventors aren't so great with words."

"Well, maybe you can invent our way out of the land of Een," Kendra suggested. "Finding Professor Bumblebean's secret tunnel just isn't working."

A smile suddenly appeared across the raccoon's masked face. "You know what, Kendra? That's a great suggestion!"

"Oh, no," Oki groaned. "What are you cooking up now, Ratchet?"

"You'll find out, my young sla—I mean, apprentice," Ratchet said, patting the tiny mouse on the head. "We'll be up late tonight—I've just had the most brilliant idea!"

Oki groaned again.

Kendra herself had to wait until the next morning to learn about Ratchet's idea. On her way to the crypt, she stopped by the raccoon's laboratory to see what her two friends had

invented. Now the thing about Ratchet's inventions, as Kendra knew, was that they were rarely practical. There was his weather clock, for example, which released a sample of the weather outside so that you knew how to dress in the morning. But the problem was that it worked almost *too* well, and soon, Eens all over Faun's End were being awoken by gusts of gale-force winds, or tidal waves of rain, or—in one unfortunate case—an avalanche of snow.

"I just need to work out the kinks," Ratchet had said at the time, which was pretty much what he said whenever one of his inventions experienced a hiccup.

Of course, nothing could have prepared Kendra for Ratchet's latest harebrained plan. As she came into the raccoon's yard, what should she see but a giant firecracker pointing up towards the clouds! A long fuse trailed out behind the firecracker, but the most frightening part of the device was the fact that Oki was strapped to a tiny seat at the top. The little mouse was dressed in a small cap and goggles, and he was wearing a long yellow scarf. Ratchet was about to light the fuse with a long match.

"RATCHET!" Kendra exclaimed. "What do you think you're doing?"

"Oh, hi," the raccoon greeted her with a wave of his black paw. "You're just in time to witness our great experiment."

"Experiment?" Kendra gasped. "Is that what you call this?"

"No," Ratchet said proudly. "I call it a *cracker seat*."

"Oh, dear," Oki squeaked from his place on the rocket, high above the ground.

"Oki!" Kendra called. "Are you all right?"

"Well, I'm rather afraid of heights, and I'm not quite sure I want to fly into outer space," the mouse answered timidly.

"I told you already; you're not going into outer space," Ratchet hollered. "Just to the other side of the magic curtain. Now be a good slave and don't complain!"

"He's not your slave!" Kendra cried with exasperation. "He's your apprentice."

"Oh, yes, right," Ratchet said apologetically. "I'll get that right one of these days."

"Oki, get down from there right now!" Kendra ordered.

"But we haven't launched yet," Ratchet said.

"And you're not going to!" Kendra said, ripping the matches out of Ratchet's paws. "Really, this is the most ridiculous invention you've come up with yet! You're going to fry poor Oki with this thing."

"No, I won't," the raccoon said defensively. "You want to get out of Een, don't you?"

"But this won't do it," Kendra told him. "You can't fly over the curtain. It's like a great dome that covers us. Poor Oki will just go smashing into it. That's if he survives the . . . the . . ."

"Blast off?" Ratchet offered.

"Oh, dear," Oki squeaked again.

"What possessed you to put a rocket under Oki's tail?" Kendra demanded as the tiny mouse clambered down from the cracker seat.

"Well, think about it," Ratchet said.

"I'm trying not to," Kendra said.

"Well, your uncle did say I was full of magic perspiration," Ratchet declared in his defense.

"No, not *perspiration*," Kendra corrected with a sigh. "He said *inspiration*."

"Oh," Ratchet said, scratching his whiskery chin. "What's the difference?"

"One means you sweat a lot—the other means you have . . . er, ideas," Oki explained as he eagerly climbed down from the firecracker.

"Come on you two," Kendra said, still shaking her head. "That's enough inventing for the time being. I think we'll stick with trying to find the secret tunnel."

"Thanks, Kendra," Oki said, squeezing the girl's hand as they set off toward Faun's End and the mysterious crypt. "You saved my whiskers that time."

"I think I saved more than that," Kendra told him.

"Well," Oki said, "it's certainly not dull being Ratchet's slave—er, I mean, apprentice!"

CHAPTER 8

Oki Takes a Tumble

When Kendra and her friends arrived at the statue of the *Fallen Faun*, they found that the doorway leading to the crypt was open and waiting for them.

"Professor Bumblebean must be here already," Kendra remarked as they entered the dark and gloomy chamber. "Maybe he decided to get an early start on the day's search."

Ratchet had lit a torch, but the chamber was still very dark. They cast their eyes around the crypt to see if anything was out of order, but the peculiar artifacts—goblets and chests and small tokens—were where they had left them the day before. Along the far wall of the crypt, life-size Een statues stood in a row, staring blankly ahead, just as they had done for hundreds of years. There was no sign of Professor Bumblebean.

"Hello?" Kendra called out, giving her braids an anxious tug. "Professor Bumblebean? Are you here?"

"That's strange," Ratchet said, scratching his whiskery chin. "If he's not here, why was the door open?"

"Oh, I don't like this at all," Oki declared. "I think we should just go back outside."

"Now, now, don't fret," Ratchet said. "Just think of onions—or turnips, or whatever vegetable it is that you like so much these days."

"Wait a minute," Kendra said, putting her hand to her ear. "Do you hear something?"

They all listened. Sure enough, after a moment, they heard a strange sound: "Mumph! Umph mumph!"

"What the heck is that?" Ratchet asked, swinging his torch around in the darkness.

Then Kendra's eyes caught a shape in the corner of the room. "Ratchet," she said, "shine your torch back that way!"

The large raccoon obeyed and there, in the corner of the room, they saw a hapless-looking Een all curled up on the floor with his arms and legs tied. Quickly, they all rushed over to the poor fellow.

"Why, it's Professor Bumblebean!" Oki squeaked.

"What happened to you?" Ratchet asked.

But Professor Bumblebean's only reply was, "Mumph! Umph mumph!"

"That doesn't make any sense," the raccoon declared.

"That's because he has a gag in his mouth," Kendra said. "He can't speak properly." She quickly leaned down and began to work the gag free.

"Mumph! Umph mumph!" the professor groaned, and his eyes were wide with fright.

"Something's wrong," Oki whispered, looking frantically about the pitch-black crypt. "He's trying to warn us of something! There's someone else here."

Kendra couldn't help thinking that Oki was right. It was as if someone was watching them. She turned away from Professor Bumblebean (who was still not yet free of his gag) and stared at the row of statues that lined one wall of the crypt. But nothing seemed amiss.

"C'mon, hurry up," Ratchet urged. "We're never going to find the secret tunnel out of Een at this rate!"

Then, suddenly, Kendra saw a shadow move from behind one of the statues.

"Days of Een!" Kendra screamed with a jump. "It's Burdock Brown!"

"Aha!" the sinister Een screeched, and now he pounced out of his hiding place and stood before them. He had a triumphant gleam in his eyes and he was wielding his wizard's staff.

"What are you doing here?" Kendra demanded.

"I knew you were up to something," Burdock sneered. "So I came down here to find out what you were up to. Unfortunately, old Bumblebean wouldn't say a word . . . but thanks to the big mouth of the bungling raccoon, I now know!"

"You don't know anything!" Ratchet declared.

"Oh, but I do," Burdock gloated. "Trying to find a way out of Een, are we? Well, that's illegal! I'll soon have you all cast in the dungeon!"

"EEK!" Oki cried, and in the next minute, several things all happened at once.

The tiny mouse turned tail and ran into the dark shadows of the crypt. Burdock tried to stop him with zaps of lightning from his staff, but was only able to singe the frightened mouse's tail. Ratchet tried to avoid the zaps too, but he ended up falling backwards, on top of Professor Bumblebean, who mumbled "Mumph! Umph mumph!" As for Kendra, the only thing she could think to do was to wind up and kick Burdock as hard as she could in the shin.

"OUCH!" the vile Een screeched, dropping his staff to the floor with a clatter.

"Serves you right!" Kendra told him.

"Well, you'll pay for it," Burdock sneered, reaching out to grab hold of Kendra with a bony hand. "You're a pesky little girl," he hissed. "I knew you were trouble from the very beginning! Now, everyone will see it too!"

"I don't think so!" cackled a voice from the darkness.

It was Jinx! Before Kendra had time to think, the speedy grasshopper shot out of the shadows like an arrow, feet first, and kicked Burdock right in the back. The dreadful Een released Kendra and fell to the ground in a heap.

"Arg!" Burdock scowled and reached out for his staff, which was still lying on the ground. Quickly Jinx kicked it across the floor, out of his reach. "You know what your problem is?" Jinx retorted. "You don't have a captain to do your fighting for you! Oh yes, that's right. I was your captain—until you fired me!"

"I'll get a new one," Burdock scowled. "One that isn't a critter! And as soon as I call him, he'll lock you all in chains and cart you to the dungeon. It's against the law to leave Een! You're all criminals!"

"Not if I have anything to do with it," Ratchet declared, once he had finally untangled himself from Professor Bumble-bean. He quickly produced a small pouch from inside his vest.

"What's that?" Burdock demanded.

"I call it *Snore Galore*," Ratchet replied. He thrust his paw inside and quickly cast a handful of the glittery dust upon Burdock. In an instant, their nemesis was asleep.

"What in the world is *Snore Galore*?" Kendra asked.

"It's a sleeping powder, of course," the raccoon replied. "I've been developing a whole line of new magical powders. You should see some of them!"

"Never mind that right now," Jinx said. "How long will this *Snore Galore* last?"

"Oh, he'll sleep until next week," Ratchet said confidently.

"Well, then, we better find the tunnel before he wakes up," Jinx said.

"First things first," Kendra declared. "Let's untie the poor professor."

"Mumph! Umph mumph!" Professor Bumblebean mumbled in agreement.

Jinx bent down over the professor and tugged the gag out of his mouth. Then, with a flick of her claws, she cut the ropes that bound his hands and legs.

"I do say!" the professor remarked. "That feels much better. Thank you, Jinx."

"No problem," the grasshopper returned. "Though I think I like you a lot better when you can't speak!"

"My word, what do you mean by that?" Professor Bumblebean asked, but Jinx just smiled.

"Come on," Kendra told her friends. "We have to find Oki. He disappeared when Burdock showed up."

Jinx lit more torches and soon they were all peering into the dim corners of the crypt in search of the timid little mouse.

It was Kendra who at last found her friend. He was lying flat on the stone floor, for in his haste, he had fallen and knocked himself out. As Kendra came upon him, he was just waking up.

"Oh, my head," Oki groaned.

"What happened?" Kendra asked, kneeling down beside her friend.

"I tripped on some sort of iron rod that was sticking out of the floor," the mouse replied.

"Iron bar?" Kendra asked.

She reached over and cleared away some of the dust on the floor. She found the rod, which was the shape of an upside down **U** and was protruding from the floor like a handle—the perfect thing to trip on. Without even thinking, Kendra pulled up on the bar.

Immediately, she felt the floor of the crypt groan and rumble, as if massive stones were shifting. Then, the tiles lying ahead of them opened up to reveal a long, dark shaft.

"Oh my," Kendra gasped.

There—right beneath Oki's whiskery nose—was the secret tunnel leading to the outside world.

CHAPTER 9

Guncle Griffinskitch Casts a Spell

If you have ever looked long and hard for something that meant a lot to you, then you will know how Kendra now felt. She gazed down into the shaft in the floor and her heart gave a leap at the sight of the long staircase spiraling into the darkness. At last, they had found the way out of Een. At last they had found the way to begin the search for the Door to Unger.

"Come on," Kendra said excitedly as she helped little Oki to his feet. "We have to get the others and go tell Uncle Griffinskitch!"

Within the hour, they were all back at the yew tree house, sitting at the table and describing their morning's adventures to the old wizard. Now that they had discovered a way to the outside world, Kendra assumed that they would spend the next few days making preparations for their long quest. But Uncle Griffinskitch had other ideas.

"We leave tonight," the whiskered wizard declared after all was told. "We mustn't risk Burdock waking up and alerting the rest of the council. Otherwise, we may all find ourselves in chains."

"Over my dead green body," Jinx said, gritting her teeth.

"Well, that might be," said Uncle Griffinskitch, "but the important thing is to be on our way. You've all been outside of the magic curtain before, so you know what to pack. Gather your things and meet back here at midnight."

For Kendra, the next few hours were a whirlwind of activity. There seemed so many things to do, yet so little time in which to do them. She set to work preparing for the long journey ahead. First she rubbed down her traveling boots with oil so that they would stay waterproof. Then she mended the holes in her long green cloak. Next, she packed her clothes and a few important supplies into her small knapsack. Somehow, she even found a moment to help Oki write a note to his parents, telling them that he was off to search for rare mushrooms in the distant Hills of Wight with his master.

"Do you think it's wrong to lie?" Kendra asked her friend, for while the Hills of Wight were far away from Faun's End, they were still safely tucked inside the magic curtain of Een.

"I don't see how we have a choice," Oki said. "It's illegal to leave Een now, so we can't tell anyone what we're about to do. Besides, my parents will be less worried this way. Remember the last time I left Een? My mother kept imagining that I would end up as lunch meat for some terrible monster."

"Well, that should make you feel better this time, then," Kendra said.

"Not really," the little mouse said. "I'll still worry!"

Before Kendra knew it, night had fallen and the small company of adventurers was creeping through the town of Faun's End, towards the crypt and the secret tunnel. Kendra could not help to think of how different this adventure was from the last time she had left the land of Een, the previous summer. Then, she and the others had been seen as would-be heroes, specifically chosen to go and search for one of Een's most precious treasures: the Box of Whispers. *But everything's turned on its head now*, Kendra thought. *Now, we have to sneak out of Een. Now, we're outlaws.*

Outlaws or not, they encountered the first problem of their new adventure the moment they arrived at the crypt, for there was no sign of Burdock Brown. Of course, they had expected to find the ornery Een fast asleep, right where they had left him.

"Ratchet, I thought you said this powder of yours was supposed to keep him asleep for days," Uncle Griffinskitch said.

"Well, I guess I'm still working out the kinks," Ratchet explained, scratching his head. "I guess old Browny woke up."

"Humph," Uncle Griffinskitch muttered, and Kendra knew it was the type of humph that meant he wasn't at all fond of kinks. "Let's make haste," the old wizard said. "I suspect Burdock will soon be on his way to stop us."

The old wizard had no sooner spoken, when they all heard a clatter on the stairs that led down to the crypt.

"Halt in the name of the Law!" someone shouted. They could hear a great many footsteps headed towards them.

"Eek!" Oki squeaked. "It's him! It's Burdock!"

"And it sounds like he's brought help," Kendra added.

"To the tunnel!" Uncle Griffinskitch ordered.

Quickly they crossed the floor of the dark crypt. Kendra had closed the door to the secret tunnel before leaving last time, so now she knelt to the floor and quickly pulled up on the lever. The floor shifted and creaked as the shaft opened again.

Jinx bounded into the dark tunnel, clenching a torch in one of her many hands. "Come on, everyone!" she called. "I'll lead the way."

They all crawled through the narrow opening in the floor, with Uncle Griffinskitch and Kendra the last to enter. Just as her long braids brushed the lip of the hole, Kendra could hear Burdock and his guards enter the crypt.

"Traitors!" Burdock shouted angrily, and Kendra could imagine his one eyebrow arching furiously on his forehead. "Come back here!"

"Humph!" muttered Uncle Griffinskitch, and with that, he pulled a small lever from the inside of the tunnel and the hatch closed above them.

There was a series of loud thumps on the floor above their heads.

"What was that?" Kendra asked her uncle as they crouched together in the darkness of the stairs.

"Burdock's guards threw their spears at us," the wizard replied. "I guess I closed the hatch just in time."

Kendra turned and gazed down the stairwell. Jinx had already led Oki, Ratchet, and Professor Bumblebean into the darkness and she could only see the faint glow of the grasshopper's torch, far below. She guessed that they had started descending the stairs without realizing that she and Uncle Griffinskitch weren't right behind them. Still, Kendra waited with her uncle, for now she could hear more footsteps above them—Kendra knew it was Burdock and his Een guards running across the crypt to find the lever for the hatch. She clutched at her braids nervously.

"Don't worry," Uncle Griffinskitch said, as if he could read her thoughts. "Even if they find the lever, we'll be long on our way."

With these words, the old wizard waved a wrinkled hand over his staff to make it glow like a torch and began leading the way down the long, stone stairs.

Now that she could see better, Kendra caught her breath. The stairs spiraled downward like a corkscrew with no railing or wall on either side. Peering cautiously over the edge, she could not see any bottom to the long sheer drop. One wrong step would mean a plummet to the death. Complicating this treacherous journey was the fact that each step was quite long—certainly, the stairs had not been built by Eens—and Kendra and her uncle almost had to hop from one step to the next.

"Oh, dear," Kendra murmured with a gulp. "Poor Oki must be terrified!"

As for Uncle Griffinskitch, he did not seem bothered at all by the steepness of their path. He marched steadily downward, grunting here and there and never letting go of Kendra's arm. Kendra felt as though the chasm was enormous. The air was stale and cold and each time Uncle Griffinskitch

grunted, the sound echoed. Kendra pulled her green cloak tighter to her shoulder and tried to concentrate on the faint light of her uncle's staff.

After what seemed like hours, Kendra and Uncle Griffinskitch reached the bottom of the mighty chasm. Here, the stairs ended in a sort of dock that jutted out over a vast underground river. The water looked deep and inky as it slowly wound its way down a long horizontal tunnel.

The others were waiting at the end of the dock.

"What now?" Jinx asked as Kendra and her uncle joined them. "didn't bring a boat and I think we're going to swim."

"You won't catch me in that water," Oki squeaked. "Not for all the turnips in Turnipville."

"Turnipville?" Professor Bumblebean asked. "I do say, where is that?"

"I just made it up," Oki said with a shrug.

"What are we going to do, Uncle Griffinskitch?" Kendra asked, toying with her braids.

"Humph," the old wizard muttered, and Kendra knew it was the type of humph that meant he had to think.

The white-bearded Een sat down on the cold, rickety dock, closed his eyes, and clasped his hands in front of him. Kendra and the others knew enough to be quiet so he could think. They moved off into the distance and waited glumly in the darkness. After awhile, Uncle Griffinskitch opened his sharp blue eyes and said simply, "Kendra, find me a walnut."

It seemed a strange request, but the girl did indeed have a small supply of nuts in her pouch. Of course, these were Een-sized nuts, and quite tiny. Kendra passed one to her uncle. He eyed it carefully in the light of his torch then placed it on the ground and cracked it open with a heavy stamp of his foot.

"Do you really think this is the right time to stop and snack?" Ratchet asked the wizard.

"Humph," Uncle Griffinskitch snorted. "You will see, Ring-tail, how well magic works when one *does* work out the kinks."

With that, Uncle Griffinskitch picked a perfect half shell of the walnut from the ground and cleaned it out with his finger. Then he waved his staff over the shell and murmured an incantation. Almost immediately—and to everyone's great surprise—the shell grew to an enormous size and sat wobbling at the edge of the dock.

"My word!" Professor Bumblebean exclaimed, fussing with his glasses as if he didn't quite believe what he was seeing. "What do we have here?"

"That," Uncle Griffinskitch said, "is our boat."

CHAPTER 10

Attack of the Terrible Skerpent

Even the most steadfast vessel is of little use without a way to steer it, and now Kendra and her companions realized a new problem: They were without oars for their boat.

Thankfully, Jinx soon solved this problem, for near the dock there stood a row of large stone Fauns, and each figure held a long wooden pole. The wood had not rotted, even after all these years, and from these poles, Jinx was able to fashion a pair of crude oars.

"They're not the prettiest," the tiny grasshopper declared, "but they'll certainly do the job."

The small band of adventurers was soon on their way down the dark, underground river. The water was shallow and murky and had a slow current, so each passenger had to share in the duties of rowing the walnut boat. This they did dutifully, each of them thinking that the tunnel would soon come to an end and lead them to the ground above. But it did not. The river wound ever-forward into the darkness, hour after hour. Indeed, there seemed to be no end in sight.

"I wonder if we'll ever see light again," Oki murmured, for he was already growing quite terrified of the darkness.

"Not to fear, little one," Professor Bumblebean said, rather cheerfully. "All roads come to an end."

The professor had finished his turn at the oars and now had his nose buried in one of the many books he had packed. Kendra wondered how he could read in the dim light cast by the single torch that they kept burning to guide their way, but the professor did not seem at all bothered. He loved to read and rarely found a reason that was good enough to inhibit his passion. Indeed, even though they were going on a long journey, Professor Bumblebean had found it fit to pack a great many books, parchments, maps, and other such things to study along the way. Kendra could hardly believe that the frail Een could carry such a load, but carry it, he did.

"Who built the dock and the stairs leading up into the crypt?" Kendra asked the professor. "The steps were much too big for tiny Een feet."

"I do agree," Professor Bumblebean said, quite pleased to address Kendra's curiosity. "Why, it was the Fauns, of course, who constructed the works. This book that I am now reading, *Myths and Legends of Flavius Faun, the Founder of Faun's End*, explains that Flavius came through the tunnel many hundreds of years ago with a small band of followers. Their journey came to an end in our tiny town—and hence the reason it is called Faun's End. Afterwards, I suppose the ancient Eens found it only appropriate to bury Flavius above the tunnel."

"I wish they would have buried him above an open road, with sky over it," Oki declared. "Then we wouldn't be stuck under here, on this underground river."

"Why that hardly makes sufficient sense," Professor Bumblebean declared. "One can hardly build a road over sky."

"I know it," Oki said. "But I wish it anyway."

Their journey up the river continued on through the night and into the day (you will remember, they had begun their journey at midnight). The river sometimes twisted and turned, and sometimes it forked in different directions. Since they had no map of the tunnel, they had no advice as to which fork to take in these instances, but Uncle Griffinskitch always made the decision with confidence, so Kendra trusted that the old wizard was relying on his magic to guide them.

The days turned into a week. Really, time had little meaning, for they could not see when the sun had set or the moon had risen; it was one long, dark journey. But they had to make the best of it. They had not packed a great deal of food, for they had hoped to forage for seeds and berries in the outside world. Of course, there were no berries or seeds to be found on the long underground river, so mostly they nibbled at their supply of Een cake, which, in all truth, is a poor name for it because it is nothing more than dry, bitter bread made from the nectar of dandelions. Still, Een cake lasts a very long time, so it is the perfect thing when one is going on a journey to distant lands.

The members of the company took turns sleeping and tried not to get on each other's nerves in the confines of the small boat—for indeed, as a nut, the boat was quite large, but as a place to live in, it was incredibly crowded. They amused themselves in the ways they knew how. Professor Bumblebean delighted in reading his various books, of course, and attempted to continue Jinx's reading lessons, though the tiny grasshopper much preferred to spend her time sharpening her weapons. Ratchet dreamed of strange new inventions, and Oki murmured fretfully about turnips, hoping that this practice would help him forget his fears. Uncle Griffinskitch spent long hours sitting at the front of the walnut boat, his eyes closed in concentration.

As for Kendra, she passed the time imagining what it would be like to find her family, at long last. Now that she had been given the clue of the Door to Unger, she knew she was closer than ever to finding them. If she could only find this mysterious door, then she would discover the truth about her family. At least, that is what Oroook the Unger had told her. Of course, he had also told her that she had the strange mark of a star on her hand, but no matter how hard Kendra studied her palm, the mark was invisible to her.

Then early one morning (at least it seemed early to Kendra; she really couldn't tell) the walnut boat was jostled so roughly that it nearly capsized. In normal circumstances, Kendra would have been frightened; but in truth, she had grown so bored, that she was ready to welcome any excitement.

"What happened?" she asked eagerly.

"Something just bumped us," Jinx declared, jamming one of the long poles into the thick mud at the bottom of the river, so as to stop the boat.

"EEK!" Oki squeaked. "What's a 'something'?"

"Maybe it was a turnip," Ratchet said in jest.

"Shh," Uncle Griffinskitch said, leaning far over the boat. He waved his hand over his staff, and the staff cast a light over the dark water. "Did you see it, Jinx?"

"No," the grasshopper replied sternly. "But I sure felt it."

"Humph," the old wizard muttered.

For a time, everyone was leaning over the boat and silently scanning the dark surface of the water. Then, suddenly, Kendra saw a long shadow streak through the murky depths of the river.

Oki saw it too. "Look!" the little mouse squealed, pointing a paw to the water. "I see scales!"

"Scales?" the professor asked. "I do say! We must have encountered some fish."

But this was no fish—that much became clear in the very next instant when a terrible creature came shooting up from the ink-black water. Now, to a human such as you or me, this creature would have seemed large—but to Kendra and her companions, it was simply enormous, a horrible beast that reared out of the water, a tangle of eyes and teeth. It was long like a whip, and it had a thick body covered in copper-colored scales; indeed, in many ways, it was like a snake. But unlike most snakes, this one had three heads.

"Why, it's a skerpent!" Professor Bumblebean declared, quickly flipping through one of his books.

"A what?" Kendra gasped, her eye fixed on the monster.

"A skerpent!" the professor repeated. He had now found the proper place in his book and happily read out the following passage: "Skerpent are nocturnal creatures, preferring to live underground in moist or wet environments. In a group, they are known as a coil. Their diet consists of—"

"Oh, do shut it!" Jinx scowled, drawing her sword. "Skerpent or not, this thing looks like it means business!"

The tiny grasshopper was right, for at that moment, the beast lunged towards the walnut boat with all three heads, its jaws snapping, eyes gleaming, tongues flickering.

"EEK!" Oki screamed. "Don't think of turnips! Don't think of turnips!" In his fright, he reached out and grabbed hold of the nearest thing he could find—which, in this case, happened to be old Uncle Griffinskitch's beard. In the next moment the old wizard and the mouse had tumbled to the bottom of the boat in a great pile.

"Days of Een!" Uncle Griffinskitch exclaimed. "How will I save us now?"

But Jinx was on the job. Just before the skerpent could strike, Jinx launched herself at the creature and drove it away from the boat with a mighty kick of her long back legs. Both grasshopper and beast plunged into the river, disappearing beneath the surface.

"Jinx!" Kendra cried. "Where are you?"

Only a moment later the giant skerpent burst out of the water, the feisty Jinx riding its thick coils.

"That's the way, Jinx!" Professor Bumblebean shouted, leaning over the boat. "It says in this book that skerpents don't like confrontation!"

"Do you mind?" Jinx called back. "I'm kind of busy here!"

She now struck down at the skerpent with every weapon she had. None would seem to break through the leviathan's strong scales, but the skerpent now let loose a horrific squeal that seemed to shake the entire cavern. It thrashed madly about the water, causing a tidal wave that sent the tiny walnut boat—and all its occupants—hurtling against the rocky shore.

Like any good nut, the boat was shattered and Kendra and her companions were sent sprawling across the rocks. No one seemed hurt, but even as they crawled from the wreckage, Jinx continued to wage battle with the terrible skerpent. It snapped at her with each of its three heads, and yet the speedy grasshopper seemed to avoid every attack, jumping here and there and thrusting at the skerpent's writhing body with her swords.

It was a noble fight, but at last the skerpent was able to wrap each of its three long tongues around Jinx. Soon the skerpent's angry heads were all pulling the grasshopper in different directions. It was like a game of tug-of-war—and Jinx was the rope.

Then, just as it seemed as if the tiny grasshopper had met her end, a loud, sharp voice cut through the darkness of the tunnel.

"Who dares to play with the pet of his royal majesty, King Reginaldo IV?"

CHAPTER 11

The Master of Keys

At the sound of this strange voice, everyone turned to see a most remarkable character waddle into the dim light of the tunnel. One glimpse told Kendra that he was none other than a Dwarf, for she had met one on her last journey into the outside world. Now, it might seem odd for an Een such as Kendra to call this creature a Dwarf, for indeed, he was at least twice as big as she. But of course, to you or me, he would have appeared quite small—but a Dwarf he certainly was, for he had a gray bushy beard, large ears, and a long nose. The most peculiar aspect of the figure, however, was that he was covered from head to foot in keys. These hung from his arms and his waist and even from his beard, so that he jingled and jangled as he moved.

"Poor little Pooky-Wooens," the Dwarf exclaimed as he approached the edge of the shore and looked upon the skerpent. "Have they been playin' rough with ya?"

"Rough!" cried Jinx, who was still ensnared within the knot of tongues. "Who do you think is in trouble here, anyway?"

"Eh, what's that?" the Dwarf asked, looking upon Jinx as if he was just noticing her predicament. "Oh, righty! Okay, Pooky-Wooens, ya can let the little shrimp go."

At once, the skerpent dropped Jinx, and she fell into the water with a splash. The skerpent cast a glare in the direction of Kendra and the others before slithering off into the dark corners of the tunnel. As for Jinx, she swam to shore to join her friends, an angry scowl upon her face.

The Dwarf now approached Kendra and the rest of the company and looked upon them with interest. He had a gleam in his eye, and Kendra for one could not tell if his intentions were good or ill. "Well, yer tiny folk aren't ya?" the Dwarf said after a moment. "We're used to havin' bigger sl—well, that is, we ain't used to seein' folks smaller then ourselves here in the Kingdom of Umbor."

"The Kingdom of Umbor!" Professor Bumblebean exclaimed. "Do you mean to say we have arrived in the fabled land of the Dwarves?"

"You know it, do ya?" the Dwarf asked.

"Aye," Uncle Griffinskitch replied. "We met a Dwarf on our last journey. Perhaps you have heard of him? His name is Pugglemud."

The Dwarf eyed the old wizard closely, and scratched his beard as if in deep thought. He jingled as he scratched, and now that she was closer, Kendra had a better look at the character's strange assortment of keys. These were keys of all kinds: some were long, some were short, some were new and sparkling, some were old and tarnished. It seemed as if the Dwarf had a key for every type of lock she could imagine.

"Well, I don't know any Pugglemud," the Dwarf said after another moment. "But I'll have to bring ya before King Reginaldo now. I can't be leavin' ya to be wanderin' around his dominions."

"And who are you?" Uncle Griffinskitch asked the Dwarf.

"You can call me Crumpit," the Dwarf replied. "I am the Key Master, on the account that I carry all these keys."

"Who would have guessed?" Jinx sneered, for she was still cross from her fight with the skerpent.

"Well, come on, then," Uncle Griffinskitch said to Crumpit. "Lead us on to your king."

The company quickly gathered their belongings, which were still strewn about the rocks from their fight with the skerpent, and after a few moments, were in line behind the peculiar Key Master.

"I'm pretty sure I could invent a better system for this fellow to carry all those keys," Ratchet remarked. "Add that to the list, Oki."

"The list of what?" the tiny mouse asked.

"The list of all my great ideas," Ratchet replied. "Aren't you keeping a list? Just what kind of slave are you?"

"Ratchet!" Kendra exclaimed as she shouldered her pack. "How many times do I have to tell you? He's your APPRENTICE. Not your slave."

"Geesh," Ratchet muttered. "The way you fuss over words, you'd think you were Bumblebean, Kendra."

"You can all jus' quit yer chatter," Crumpit called over his shoulder. "We have a bit of a journey ahead of us."

The Dwarf led them down the tunnel a short way before coming to a stop before a section of the rocky wall. To Kendra, the wall seemed no different than any other part of the tunnel, but Crumpit now unhooked a key from just below his knee and inserted it into a small hole in the rock. Then with a groan, a section of the wall pulled away, revealing a dark set of steps.

"Down we go," Crumpit said.

"Oh, great turnips," Oki murmured to Kendra. "Aren't we ever going to start going *upwards*?"

"It's okay," Kendra said, taking the mouse's paw. "Just stay close to me."

The stairs seemed to wind down into the very center of the earth, but they had only taken a dozen or so steps when Crumpit suddenly stopped, bent to his knees, and took a small silver key from under his armpit. This he inserted into a small slot in the step just ahead of him. He turned the key with a click and then lifted up the step to reveal another set of stairs, leading even further down.

This time they took the steps all the way to the bottom, where they ended in a small round chamber. There were eight doors in the room. Without a moment's hesitation, Crumpit went to the door that was second from their left and produced a small rusted key from behind his ear.

"There are so many doors in this place," Kendra told Uncle Griffinskitch, as the Key Master fiddled with the lock. "Maybe one of them is the Door to Unger."

"It's unlikely, Kendra," Uncle Griffinskitch murmured. "But perhaps this King Reginaldo will be able to shed some light on the mystery."

"If we ever get to him," Kendra remarked. "This place seems to be bursting with tricks."

"Indeed," Professor Bumblebean agreed. "I do say, Mr. Crumpit, are you not worried that we will remember this secret set of doors into the land of Umbor? You haven't even blindfolded us!"

"Ya won't remember it at all," Crumpit replied, finally opening the door and leading them through to the passage beyond. "It's a long way, and it takes a lifetime fer a Key Master to remember everything along the way. And one wrong turn can mean disaster."

"What do you mean?" Kendra asked.

"Well, fer example, if we took the wrong door back that way we would have ended up in a nest of skerpents," Crumpit explained, pausing to return his key to its rightful place on his body. "And those ones aren't friendly like our little Pooky-Wooens."

"Oh, dear," Oki murmured. "I'd sure hate to meet a *big* Pooky-Wooens."

"It's no account anyway," Crumpit muttered. "I doubt much you'll be comin' back this way."

"And what do you mean by that, Crumpit?" Uncle Griffinskitch asked.

"Eh? What's that?" the Dwarf asked. "Oh, nothin'. Now, c'mon, we're just gettin' started."

With this remark, the strange fellow continued on his way, leading the small company through the network of caverns and unlocking doors with his collection of keys. This activity continued for several hours. Sometimes the doors were plain to see, and sometimes they were hidden. Some were in the floor, some were in the ceiling, and some were so tiny that the Dwarf had to crawl through on all fours (though Kendra and her friends were so small compared to Crumpit that they could just walk through normally). Once they had to cross a lake of bubbling lava on a narrow bridge of rock. Halfway across, Crumpit stopped, inserted a key into the bridge deck, and a large bucket was lowered down on a chain from the ceiling. They all climbed in and were pulled up to the next series of caverns. Kendra could only imagine what would have happened if one were to cross the length of the rock bridge. She guessed that it might collapse 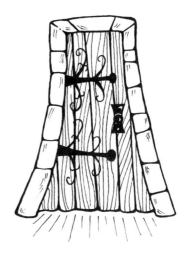 when you were almost to the other side; or maybe a terrible creature was waiting to attack any unsuspecting intruder.

In any case, Kendra realized that Crumpit was right; there was no way she could remember all the twists and turns that led to the Kingdom of Umbor. Without him to guide them, they would never find their way into—or out of—the land of Dwarves.

The trip seemed to stretch on for hour upon hour. Kendra had been so used to sitting in the boat that it was quite a bit of exercise to suddenly use her legs through such a set of stairs and tunnels, and she could tell by the grunts and groans from the rest of the party that they felt much the same, save for Jinx, who rarely seemed to tire. Kendra kept hoping that each door would mean the end of their journey, but still the strange Key Master continued on, opening door after door with his assortment of keys.

"How many doors do you think we've gone through?" Oki asked Kendra after a time.

"I've lost count, to tell the truth," Kendra replied. "Maybe a hundred."

"It feels like a thousand, if you ask me," Oki said.

In any case, a hundred or a thousand, the small party was to pass through several more doors yet before Crumpit finally brought them to a halt. Before them stood a simple door of iron and wood and the Key Master now spoke his first words in many hours.

"Well, we're here, don't ya know," he declared, reaching into his black beard and producing one last key. "On the other side of this here door is the land of Umbor."

CHAPTER 12

In the Court of King Reginaldo

You have probably never been to visit a king, let alone one who is a Dwarf. Well, let me tell you, what Dwarves may lack in grace, manners, and charm, they do their best to compensate with gold, silver, and jewels. This was something that Kendra and her friends were to discover firsthand; for now, as Crumpit unlocked the last of the doors, they passed into an enormous world of bedazzling riches.

At first, Kendra mistakenly thought that they had come to the surface of the earth, for the space was so vast that it went as far as her tiny eyes could see. It was only when she looked upward that she noticed a vaulted ceiling, high above them.

"Why, we're not outside at all!" the tiny Een girl declared.

"No indeed," Professor Bumblebean said. "It's one gigantic subterranean cavern and, as I've read in my books, it houses the entire Kingdom of Umbor."

"And what a kingdom!" Ratchet murmured with a low whistle. "Everything here seems to be made of gold!"

Kendra could not have said it much better herself. Everywhere she looked, she was met by the glimmer of gold. The streets were paved with gold stone. The houses were built with gold bricks. Even the trees were gold, with gold bark and leaves made from large green emeralds. Kendra turned slowly around to take in the sights, rubbing her eyes at the brilliance. After the darkness of the tunnels, the glimmering wealth of Umbor was quite blinding.

"Well, c'mon now," Crumpit declared. "I reckon I should present ya to his majesty."

They set off through the golden streets, the Key Master leading the way with a noisy jingle. They could now see a great many Dwarfs bustling about, and many of them stopped to stare at the small party.

"I reckon most Dwarves ain't see no Eens before," Crumpit commented.

"I do say," Professor Bumblebean remarked as he looked about. "Don't you have any women or children here, in the Kingdom of Umbor? All of your fine citizens seem to be men."

"Of course, we got women and children," Crumpit replied. "Why, here's a playground of younguns right here on yer left."

"Why, they all have beards!" Kendra declared.

"Of course they do," Crumpit said. "Every Dwarf has one! Even younguns!"

"I ought to invent an easy way for these folks to shave," Ratchet said, scratching his chin thoughtfully. "Add that to the list, Oki."

"I haven't had time to start a list yet," the mouse said.

"Well, what in the name of turnips have you been doing?" the raccoon asked as they ambled down the street.

"I've been kind of busy trying not to die," Oki explained. "You know, what with the bottomless stairs, the three-headed skerpent, and all the rest."

"Excuses, excuses," Ratchet muttered.

Before long they arrived at the palace of King Reginaldo. Unlike the rest of the buildings in the cavern, which were short and squat, the palace was tall and graceful, with golden walls and gleaming panes of silver glass. Crumpit led them up some stairs to a pair of tall golden doors that were studded with large red rubies. The Dwarf unlatched a key from his elbow and used it to knock on one of the doors.

"Eh?" came a scratchy voice from behind the door. "Who's that knockin'?"

"Why, it's me, the Key Master," Crumpit replied.

"Well, whatcha want?" the gatekeeper asked. "Shouldn't ya be patrollin' the tunnels and keepin' the locks oiled?"

"I've got some new sl—well, that is, I've got some folk for King Reginaldo to meet," Crumpit replied.

"Well, that's different now, ain't it?" the gatekeeper said with a new cheer in his voice. In the next moment the massive doors creaked open and they were met by an old hunched Dwarf. He had a long gray beard and he wore a large pair of square spectacles.

"Strange sl—I mean, folk, ya have here," the gatekeeper said to Crumpit.

"They're Eens, don't ya know," the Key Master declared. "Now go and announce us to King Reginaldo."

"I will indeed," the gate-keeper replied, and Kendra could not help but to notice a twinkle in his eyes as he scurried away to do his duty.

"How long will we have to wait?" Uncle Griffinskitch asked Crumpit.

"Not long," the Key Master replied. "King Reginaldo likes to meet folk."

Sure enough, it was only a few minutes later when the gatekeeper returned, rubbing his hands together with glee. "C'mon then," he said. "His majesty awaits."

They now walked through the golden doors and found themselves in a grand hall. A long golden carpet ran down the center of the room, ending at the throne of the Dwarf king. Dwarves lined either side of the carpet, and presently, they raised trumpets to their lips and filled the hall with the blare of music.

After the trumpets quieted, one of the Dwarf courtiers proclaimed, "Welcome to the court of his Royal Majesty, King Reginaldo IV, Ruler of the Kingdom of Umbor and Grand Lord over all Underground Dominions."

"What a lot of pomp for a bunch of scoundrels," Jinx remarked.

"Humph," Uncle Griffinskitch muttered, and Kendra thought it was the type of humph that meant he quite agreed.

92

When they reached the end of the carpet, they stopped and bowed before the throne, which, of course, was made of gold and beset with jewels. And yet, Kendra hardly noticed these riches, for it was the figure sitting in the throne that commanded her attention. The Dwarf king was fat and squat, with a red beard and a sharp nose. He was dressed head to foot in gold, with golden boots, golden robes, and a tall golden crown upon his head. The most noticeable aspect of the king's wardrobe, however, was the belt that encircled his waist. The belt had been fashioned from a wide strip of gold and sparkled with rubies and sapphires.

Kendra looked upon the Dwarf king with curiosity. She had never met a king, and yet somehow this character seemed familiar. She just couldn't quite put her finger on it . . .

Then the king spoke.

"Well, if it ain't a bunch o' Een folk, don't ya know," he declared. "Come to gaze upon me gold, are ya? Tee hee!"

"Why, Pugglemud!" Kendra exclaimed. "It's you!"

There was no mistaking the voice of the Dwarf they had met during their search for the Box of Whispers. When Kendra had first met Pugglemud, he had been dressed all in rags, so it was difficult to recognize him draped in gold. But it was him all right; now, upon closer inspection, Kendra could see the real Pugglemud through all the finery. His bushy red beard was in desperate need of a trim and his fingernails were split and broken and covered in grime. All his luxurious clothes could not disguise the fact that, at heart, he was just a slob.

"Eh?" the king muttered in response to Kendra's exclamation. "What's that? I ain't go by Pugglemud no more. I be his majesty, King Reginaldo the—,"

93

"Yes, we know," Jinx interrupted. "Ruler of the everything and dominions of dirt and all that rot. But you're still Pugglemud to us. Or have you completely forgotten our adventures in the Castle of Krodos? Remember, you left us to tangle with that dragon all on our own."

"Ahem," the Dwarf king grunted. "Well, of course I 'member all those grand times we had together, don't ya know. Though I don't quite know what yer talkin' about with that dragon an' such. As I 'member it, I jus' about saved yer skins."

"Humph," Uncle Griffinskitch muttered.

"I think all this gold has gone to your head," Jinx said.

"Gold! Tee hee!" Pugglemud giggled, but after a moment, he recovered from his mirth and a stern expression came to his face. "The point bein'," he said (and now he stood up in his throne and hooked his thumbs in his magnificent gold belt so that all could see it), "I be known as King Reginaldo now. And you'll be callin' me that."

Pugglemud gazed down upon them as if he expected something to happen. It was as if, Kendra thought, he was waiting for them to shout out "King Reginaldo" all at once—and, in truth, part of her felt compelled to do just that. In fact, she suddenly felt a strange loyalty to the Dwarf king, and she started to fall to her knees.

Then Uncle Griffinskitch thumped his staff against the gold floor, and the soft thump broke Kendra's momentary trance.

"Humph," Uncle Griffinskitch muttered. "I can see you have some magic at work in your court, *King*,"—and here Kendra found herself gazing upon the Dwarf's belt—"But remember: You are not the only one who is able to cast such enchantment. Or do I need to remind you of your trousers?"

Kendra muffled a giggle as she recalled the time when they had first met Pugglemud. The Dwarf had not believed in Uncle Griffinskitch's magic then, but to prove his wizardry, the old Een had caused Pugglemud's trousers to start on fire.

"Well, ahem," the Dwarf king muttered, eyeing Uncle Griffinskitch's staff with caution. "There ain't no need to go bringin' that up. We're just all old pals after all."

"Indeed," Uncle Griffinskitch grunted.

"But Pugglemud—I mean King Reginaldo," Kendra stammered, "Why are you, I mean—er, how did you—,"

"What she's trying to say," Jinx interrupted, "is how in the name of Een did you ever become a king? The last time we saw you, you were sitting in the rubble of the castle of Krodos with every monster known to Eenkind coming toward you to get its share of gold."

"Gold!" Pugglemud repeated, giggling so that all could see his gold-capped teeth. "Tee hee! Ah, yes, all that wonderful gold. Tee hee! Well, that's a tale fer sure. But perhaps it'd be better fer another time, don't ya know. What about you wee folks? I reckon yer still lookin' fer that fancy-smancy treasure of yers, eh? The box of what's-it-now?"

"Humph," Uncle Griffinskitch muttered. "We found our Box of Whispers. We're on a quest of another kind."

"Eh, an' what's that?" Pugglemud asked. "Ya ain't come to steal all me gold, have ya now?"

"I do say!" Professor Bumblebean declared. "What would Eens do with such treasure?"

"Swim in it, of course," Pugglemud declared. "That's what us Dwarves do."

"We're not interested in gold," Uncle Griffinskitch told the Dwarf gravely. "We're searching for a door."

"Well, we got a lot o' doors about here," Pugglemud said, rubbing his chin thoughtfully. "I'll sell ya one if ya like."

"Humph," Uncle Griffinskitch muttered, and Kendra could tell that it was the type of humph that meant the old wizard was growing impatient.

"It's a special door we're looking for," Kendra explained to the Dwarf king. "It's called the Door to Unger."

"Well I ain't ever heard of no such door," Pugglemud said. "And I ain't ever heard of a land of Unger either. Them critters ain't got no proper kingdom like me, King Reginaldo IV. So how can there be a door to a place that don't exist no how?"

"Aye," Uncle Griffinskitch returned wearily. "But we seek the door nonetheless."

"What ya need to do is find some Ungers," Pugglemud said, leaning forward in his throne. He had a strange gleam in his eye, reminding Kendra of the look that she had seen in the gatekeeper.

"And I suppose you know where to find some?" Jinx asked.

"Maybe I do, maybe I don't," Pugglemud replied mysteriously. "But first things first. I don't want ya to be thinkin' that King Reginaldo don't know how to treat guests. We'll have ya come to the royal hall fer some grub tonight, don't ya know."

"But we need to be on our way," Kendra said with an anxious tug on her long braids. "We have to find the Door to Unger, you see. It's really urgent, and—"

"What's that?" Pugglemud said, his face going red. "I suppose the hospitality of the Dwarves ain't good enough fer you Een folk?"

"No, of course it is," Uncle Griffinskitch said. "We would be happy to dine with you, *King*. My niece is just eager to complete our journey, but it certainly can wait one night."

"It's all settled then," Pugglemud said cheerfully. He snapped his greasy fingers, and a small Dwarf servant appeared before him.

"My Lord?" the Dwarf asked. He had a very short beard, and Kendra guessed that he was just a boy.

"Show these folks up to a room so that they can freshen up before grub time," Pugglemud commanded.

"As you wish, your majesty," the Dwarf boy returned with a bow.

"I don't like this one bit," Kendra whispered to Oki as they followed the servant out of the grand hall. "I just don't trust Pugglemud."

"Me, neither," Oki said. "What do you think he's up to?"

"I don't know," Kendra replied. "But something smells rotten in the land of Umbor."

"Well, I hope it's not dinner," Oki said, rubbing his furry tummy. "I'm looking forward to a decent meal tonight!"

CHAPTER 13

Dinner with the Dwarves

The Dwarf boy led Kendra and her companions to a small guest chamber in the depths of the palace. It was a rather gloomy room, for though everything in it was made of gold, there were no windows and no fresh air.

"There are only two things that Dwarves seem to prize," Professor Bumblebean said after the servant had left them. "And that is gold and darkness. I suppose it's an honor to have a room with no view."

"Humph," Uncle Griffinskitch muttered.

In any case, the weary travelers had just enough time to change their clothes and wash up before the servant boy returned to escort them to dinner. The banquet hall was a large room decorated with golden tapestries and carpets and fitted with a long table and many chairs. Of course, the table and chairs were rather too big for the tiny Eens to sit at comfortably, so Pugglemud had ordered his servants to bring in bricks of gold for each of them to sit on and, in this way, they could reach their place settings.

"Look, Kendra," Oki said, tugging at the girl's sleeve. "Even the tablecloth is made of gold."

"They must know how to spin gold into cloth here in Umbor," Kendra commented. "I guess everything really is made of gold here."

"Well, I hope they don't serve gold for dinner," Ratchet declared. "That would be too rich for my diet!" The raccoon laughed out loud at his own joke, though Kendra and Oki could only groan.

Then Pugglemud entered the room, and took his seat at the head of the table. He had changed into a golden robe with a ridiculously frilly collar, but he was still wearing his sparkling gold belt.

"Well, good evenin' to ya," Pugglemud greeted. "I hope yer all hungry, 'cause we've got quite a feast prepared for ya. But first let's have a toast, eh?" The strange Dwarf king wrapped his greasy hands around his goblet and raised it before them.

"And to what occasion or event shall we toast?" Professor Bumblebean asked.

"Why, to gold, of course!" Pugglemud replied. "Tee hee!"

"Humph," Uncle Griffinskitch muttered, but he raised his goblet all the same.

"Well, bring out the soup, I says," Pugglemud declared, and by this command, several servants scurried into the room and set a large steaming bowl before each guest.

Kendra stared into her bowl. The soup was thick and white and had a peculiar smell. "Just what is this?" she asked, making a face. "It smells like . . ."

"Turnips!" Oki squeaked.

"Ugh!" Ratchet scowled.

"Shh!" Kendra said, but luckily she, Oki, and Ratchet were sitting at the opposite end of the table from Pugglemud, so he couldn't hear their comments.

"Whoever heard of turnip soup?" Oki moaned.

"Maybe it's a Dwarf specialty," Kendra suggested.

"Let's just hold on for the next course," Ratchet said. "Maybe we'll get something better."

"No, that would be rude," Kendra said in a low voice. "We have to eat what's put before us."

"Thankfully, I have something to help us out of this predicament," Ratchet whispered. He reached into his vest and produced a small pouch.

"What's that?" Oki asked.

"I call it *Dinner Thinner*," Ratchet replied. "Just sprinkle some on your soup and it will slowly disappear. Pugglemud will think we're eating it—but we won't have to taste a drop!"

"For once, an invention I like!" Oki squeaked, and he eagerly sprinkled some of the transparent powder from the pouch onto his soup. At once, the bubbling white liquid began to shrink.

Kendra cast a glance at Pugglemud to see if he was paying any attention, but the gluttonous Dwarf was busily slurping back his own soup. With a shrug, she took some of Ratchet's powder and dashed some into her bowl. Ratchet did the same, and then all three of them pretended to lift their spoons to their mouths every few moments to make it look like they were eating.

"Good grub, eh?" Pugglemud said. "Nothin' better than a good turnip, I say!"

"The best I ever tasted," Ratchet returned, though Kendra thought he said it with a little too much enthusiasm.

"Well, there's more to come," Pugglemud said, snapping his fingers for his servants. "Bring out the salad!"

"Thank goodness," Oki whispered to Kendra and Ratchet. "Imagine it! Leafs of crispy lettuce, plum ripe tomatoes, and sticks of wonderful orange carrots!"

But no such feast arrived. Instead, the Dwarf servants began hustling in with golden platters heaped with none other than—turnips. There were purple ones, red ones, and white ones, all cut into slices and arranged together on a bed of turnips leaves.

"Ah!" Pugglemud. "Turnip salad. Me favorite, don't ya know!"

"Good thing we've got lots of *Dinner Thinner,*" Ratchet said with a sigh.

If the rest of the party was dismayed by the abundance of turnips, Kendra could not tell. They all seemed to be enjoying their dinner well enough and now Professor Bumblebean, in between bites, began to engage Pugglemud in conversation.

"I do say," the Professor declared, "will you tell us now, kind sir, how it is that you managed to escape the Castle of Krodos and arrive back here none other than a sovereign monarch?"

"Eh? Whatchya callin' me now?" Pugglemud snorted.

"Why, a king!" Professor Bumblebean replied.

"Oh, why yeah, of course," Pugglemud said. "Well, I guess I could tell ya, now that . . ."

"Now that what?" Jinx asked suspiciously.

"Eh? Oh, nothing," Pugglemud said, wiping his sleeve across his mouth after a forkful of his salad. "Jus' now that we've begun dinner. That's all."

"Humph," Uncle Griffinskitch muttered. "Well, get on with it then."

"Well, like I was sayin'," Pugglemud said, "there I was a-sittin' there in the pile of gold (tee hee!) and rubble left over after the castle was destroyed. I was jus' a mindin' me own business, of course, when these critters all closed in around me. There were them Unger gang, and Goojuns, and Krakes and all those nasty types of fellers. Well, I rolled up my sleeves and as each of those nasties came in at me, I dealt 'em each a fierce blow, don't ya know."

"Humph," Uncle Griffinskitch grunted, and now he rapped his staff loudly against the table. "I do think, *King*

Reginaldo, that we'd like to hear the truth. Why don't you tell us what *really* happened."

"I reckon I've done forget how much fun you Eens ain't," Pugglemud sighed, looking uneasily upon Uncle Griffin-skitch's staff. "Well, it ain't no account anyhoo, I reckon."

Kendra cast a look at the Dwarf king and noticed that he once again had a strange gleam in his eye. *He's acting very strangely*, she thought. *Even for Pugglemud.*

"Well, let's get goin' on the main course," Pugglemud said, interrupting Kendra's thoughts. "Then I'll be tellin' ya the whole yarn about Krodos." He snapped his greasy fingers, and now the servants began bringing in covered platters for the main course.

"Finally," Ratchet said. "Some real food."

But when he lifted the cover from his platter, what should he find but a mound of—what else?—turnips! There were slabs of roasted purple turnip, covered in steaming turnip gravy, served with a side of orange turnip mash.

"This is all your fault, Oki," Ratchet hissed at the mouse. "You think so much about turnips that you've manifested an entire feast of them."

"Well, in all fairness to Oki," Kendra said, "he's actually been trying NOT to think of turnips."

"Blah," the raccoon growled, and he broke out his pouch of *Dinner Thinner* for the third time.

As they slowly watched their dinner shrink from the magic powder, Pugglemud continued with his story.

"Well, ya see," the Dwarf said, "there I was sittin' there when the critters all come up to get me. So I tries to hide meself away in all that rubble. And there I found it, lying there in all that mess."

"Found what?" Jinx asked.

"His belt," Uncle Griffinskitch answered for the Dwarf. "It has some magic charm, doesn't it, *King*?"

"Why, of course," Pugglemud said. "I found it lyin' there in all that treasure. So I says to myself, 'Why, that there looks like a might fine belt o' gold.' And I put it on, see.

"Well, right about then, one of them Ungers come at me, but I'll be durned if he couldn't lay a claw on me. He just bounced off me. The belt protected me, see. So, I says to that feller to go on and leave me alone. And he obeyed! He jus' turned around and left me alone."

"A fine piece of enchantment, I do say," Professor Bumble-bean declared with interest. "I've never read anything about such a belt in any of my books. I wonder where this magical adornment originated."

"Well, that I ain't know," Pugglemud said. "But that dragon had collected all sorts of treasure in that castle lair of his, don't ya know. So I reckon he stole it from some wizard or another."

"Humph," Uncle Griffinskitch muttered, and Kendra could not help but to notice the concern in that humph. She knew that the old wizard was having the same thought as she: an object as powerful as the magic belt would be very danger-ous in the wrong hands. *And if anyone has the wrong hands, it's Pugglemud*, Kendra said to herself.

"This belt has allowed you to become king, hasn't it?" Jinx asked wearily. "You've got all the Dwarves under your command."

"These fellers made me king," Pugglemud declared. "I'm a hero to 'em, see. Why, us Dwarves ain't so different from you Eens. We don't like them Ungers and Orrids and such no more than you do. We've always been livin' under their shadow, scared of them nasties. But not no more. Now us Dwarves will run the show, don't ya know."

"Because you're the most powerful?" Uncle Griffinskitch asked, stretching tiredly.

"Exactly," Pugglemud replied, draining the last of his gob-let. "Oh durn—Hiccup! I done gone got the hiccups again. Now I'll have 'em for hours."

"I have something that can help you out there," Ratchet announced proudly.

"Eh? And—hiccup—what's that?" Pugglemud asked.

"Oh no," Kendra groaned. "Not another magic powder?"

"I call it *Easy Sneeze*," Ratchet explained for all to hear. "One sprinkle and you start sneezing so hard that your hiccups will stop."

"That's ridiculous," Kendra said. "Who wants to have the sneezes instead of the hiccups?"

"Well, I haven't—,"

"Yes, we know," Uncle Griffinskitch interrupted. "You haven't worked out the kinks yet."

"I think we'll just—hiccup—move onto dessert," Pugglemud said, rubbing his beard suspiciously. "Maybe that will—hiccup'—stop 'em."

"I do say," Professor Bumblebean said with a long stretch. "I do feel rather tired suddenly. I suppose a bit of dessert will hit the spot before a fine long slumber."

"Let me guess," Oki said to Pugglemud with a sigh. "Turnip ice cream?"

"Why, of course!" the Dwarf answered with glee. "Ain't any other—hiccup—kind, is there?"

CHAPTER 14

Kendra Scratches an Itch

After dinner, something continued to tug at Kendra's mind. She couldn't put her finger on it, but she knew something was terribly amiss in the land of Umbor. How to describe the feeling? It was like having an itch in the very center of your back that you just want to give a good scratch, but no matter how far you stretch, you just can't reach it. And so it was with Kendra now.

She tried to speak with her uncle about it on the way back to the guest chamber, but the old wizard had grown so tired that it was all he could do to crawl into his bed and erupt into loud snores. Jinx and Professor Bumblebean

109

had soon followed suit, and now only Kendra, Ratchet, and Oki were awake.

"I guess there's nothing like a good meal to put you to sleep," Oki observed. "Unfortunately, we didn't eat a thing!"

"Yeah, I guess it's more Een cake for us," Ratchet said, digging into his pack and handing out a handful of the dry (and now quite stale) foodstuff to his friends.

"Hmm," Kendra murmured, with a long, thoughtful tug on her braids.

"That was almost an old Griffinskitch 'humph'," Ratchet said. "What's needling you, Kendra?"

"It's Pugglemud," Kendra replied, chewing absent-mindedly on her dinner. "He's up to something."

"Of course he is," Ratchet said. "I don't know what though."

"Whatever it is, you can be sure it involves gold," Oki said, adding a "tee hee" for good measure.

"I'm going to do some exploring," Kendra announced suddenly. "Maybe I can find out something."

"Well, we're coming with you, then," Ratchet said. "All we need is a disguise."

"Why?" Kendra asked.

"You can't go poking around without a disguise," Ratchet said. "We don't want those Dwarves to see what we're up to."

"That's true," Kendra said. "Good idea."

They searched about the chamber for some costumes, doing their best to keep quiet and to not wake Uncle Griffinskitch and the others (though they seemed so deeply asleep that Kendra didn't think an earthquake would wake them). There was a tall gold-plated wardrobe in the corner of the room, and here, they found a long robe that Ratchet declared would fit their need perfectly. Then Oki sat on Kendra's shoulders, and Kendra sat on Ratchet's, and together, the three of them were the same height of a normal Dwarf. The robe covered them all quite nicely, and Oki pulled it tight around his head to disguise his whiskery face and to make it look as if he were wearing a hood.

"Well, here we go," Ratchet said, as he quietly opened the door and shuffled out of the room. "Kendra, just keep your foot off of my nose!"

"If we meet any Dwarves, you'll have to do the talking," Kendra told the raccoon. "You have the deepest voice and will sound the most like one of those rascals."

"Are you calling me a rascal?" Ratchet asked as they moved down the hallway, toward the center of the palace.

"You've been called worse," Kendra said, but before the raccoon could muster a retort, they turned the corner and encountered a Dwarf coming down the passage.

"Ornelius, you scoundrel!" the Dwarf exclaimed.

"What? Who?" Ratchet cried in surprise.

"It's me, Fiddlewick," the Dwarf said. "Why you actin' so strange, Ornelius? And where you been at? We got guard duty down in the pens. And what's more, King Reginaldo wants us to be gettin' them new cages ready down there."

"Why, I reckon I'm right here, don't ya know," Ratchet replied, now trying to use his best Dwarf voice. "Can't a feller dip in a bit o' ale, don't ya know? What's the anyhoo of it any how, don't ya know?"

"Don't overdo it," Kendra whispered, kicking the raccoon.

"Ouch!" Ratchet cried.

"Eh?" Fiddlewick asked.

"Eek!" Oki cried.

"Eh?" Fiddlewick asked again. "Jus' what's wrong with ya, Ornelius?"

"Nothen'," Ratchet said quickly.

"Come on," Kendra whispered to the raccoon. "Go with him so we can see what these pens are about."

"All right, all right," Ratchet declared. "Let's get a goin' then, don't ya know."

Fiddlewick turned and Ratchet staggered after him; Kendra knew that the raccoon was strong, but she guessed that he was starting to feel her and Oki's weight.

They wound their way through the maze of passages in the palace, traveling ever-downward. They were going even lower than where the guest chambers were, and Kendra started to shiver, though she couldn't tell if it was from a growing coldness or just from her nerves.

Thankfully, Fiddlewick didn't bother to look back or talk to them along the way, which helped them keep up their disguise. Peeking out of the robe, Kendra could see the Dwarf leading them intently ahead, breaking the silence only with the odd burp—which Ratchet tried to imitate, until she gave him another kick of warning.

"You're enjoying this far too much," she muttered.

At last they arrived at a large door that had a guard standing on duty. The guard looked like every other big-eared, scruffy-bearded Dwarf in Umbor, but it was the door that was different—for here, at last, was something that was not made of gold. Indeed, it appeared to be constructed of thick iron, and it had a massive bar set across it to block anyone from coming through from the other side. Then Kendra heard sounds coming from behind the great door. They were strange and mechanical sounds, like the banging of a thousand hammers or the hum of some great industry. They were the type of sounds that sent a chill down her spine.

"Me an' Ornelius got us the next watch in the pens," Fiddlewick said to the guard.

"Sure, ain't no difference to me," the guard returned, and with some effort, he lifted the great bar so that they could pass through.

The door swung open with a slow, heavy creak. And now, peeking out of the cloak, Kendra could see the source of the noise. Stretching before them was an immense cavern filled with the underground workings of a mine. There were handcarts for moving piles of rock laden with gold and silver. There were furnaces and smelters blazing with fire to melt the precious metals. And there were hundreds and hundreds of workers, all of them swinging pickaxes and shovels to break apart the rocks and expose the treasures of the earth.

It was hard for Kendra to see through the cloak, but there was something strangely familiar about the workers. To begin with, they were enormous—much larger than Eens, or even Dwarves, for that matter—and they grunted and moaned as their dark silhouettes bent with their activity.

"Ah, the night shift's beginned," Fiddlewick declared, interrupting Kendra's thoughts. He led them into the cavern and the guard closed the door behind them with a loud clang.

Now Kendra's tiny Een ears could hear new noises: the clinking of chains and the cracking of whips.

"Ah, there ain't no pertier sound is there, eh Ornelius?" Fiddlewick beamed, looking upon the mine workings. "The sound of slaves slavin'!"

"Slaves!" Kendra said with a gasp, but if Fiddlewick heard her, he didn't respond. Instead, he turned and led them up a rocky path that was cut into the side of the cavern. They followed (or rather, Ratchet did, for he was still carrying Kendra and Oki), and they soon found themselves on a narrow ledge that looked down upon the operation of the mine.

Kendra could feel Oki trembling. "We've got to get out of here," he squeaked.

Kendra couldn't help to agree. "Ratchet," she whispered, peeking through the cloak. "There's an outcropping of rock ahead. Duck behind it."

The raccoon did as she instructed and they were soon safely hidden from Fiddlewick's view.

"Ornelius?" they heard the Dwarf call after a moment. "Where'd ya go now? Oh, jigger it! Be that way, then. It'll be yer hide boiled in turnips, not mine, if ya don't get yer work done . . ."

His voice faded away, leaving Kendra and her friends to scramble out of their disguise. They peeked over the rocks and gazed down upon the cavern of workers—or, as Fiddlewick had called them, slaves.

"So this is how Pugglemud came into all this gold," Oki murmured. "He's used his magic belt to capture helpless slaves and make them mine these caverns."

Kendra grew faint. The sound from the slaves was so loud that she felt as if their hammers and axes were beating against her head. She clutched her collar tight about her neck, as if it would somehow shield her from the horrors before her. "This is what it means to be a slave," she said to Ratchet after a moment. "It's not about bossing Oki around."

"Those were just jokes," the raccoon said with an abashed grimace. "But it's no joke now. These fellows are in a bad way."

"But where did they all come from?" Oki asked anxiously.

Kendra crept out onto the rock ledge to afford herself a closer look.

"Careful!" Ratchet warned.

With an inquisitive tug on her braids, Kendra squinted into the darkness. Finally, her eyes began to adjust to the dim light in the cavern. Now she could better make out the crooked shapes of the slaves. She could see their twisted bodies and their ragged clothes. She could see that they were—

"Days of Een!" she gasped.

"What?" Oki cried.

Kendra could feel her whole body shake as she turned to cast a startled look at her friends.

"Ungers," she murmured.

CHAPTER 15

What They Found in the M iserable Mines

Ungers!

There were hundreds of them, a throbbing swarm of twisted bodies that stretched into the dark corners of the vast cavern, as far as Kendra's small eyes could see. And yet, she and her friends soon realized that it was not Ungers alone that populated the mines. For now, as they studied the vast underground cave, they recognized an entire menagerie of creatures under the command of the Dwarves. There were Goojuns, Izzards, Krakes, and Orrids—all the hideous monsters that Kendra had known to scuttle through her nightmares. Here in the real world, they were no less frightening, for they had crooked fangs and sharp claws. And yet, Kendra realized, these creatures could not harm her even if they wished, for they were chained head to foot, with studded collars about their necks or heavy bracelets of iron around their wrists and ankles. These, the darkest creatures of the night, were slaves.

It seemed to take Oki a moment to understand what he was looking at—an entire cave filled to the brim with monsters—but the second he did, he let out a hair-curling "EEK" and turned to dash away. Quickly, Kendra leapt after the mouse and tripped him to the ground by grabbing his tail.

"Let me go!" Oki screeched. "Great turnips!"

"Shush!" Kendra said, jumping on top of him and throwing her hand over his mouth. "You'll get us caught!"

She could feel Oki's heart fluttering like a beetle in the wind, but after a moment, his squealing quieted and Kendra lifted her hand.

"But Kendra," Oki whispered anxiously. "There are so many of them!"

"It's okay," she said, helping the mouse to his feet. "We've been through worse, haven't we? It'll be okay."

"It's an awful sight," Oki said. "Don't you have a potion or powder or something to take it all away, Ratchet?"

"I sure wish," the raccoon said with a grimace.

Kendra crept back to the rock's ledge. The last thing she wanted to do was look again upon the terrible scene, but somehow she felt that she must. *It's okay*, she told herself. *Remember, they're all chained.*

She scowled as she looked down. There were many Dwarven taskmasters throughout the mine, and these wandered about the slaves, whipping them with long cords. The clang of the slaves' hammers went without pause; Kendra thought her head would explode with the sound.

119

And now Kendra could feel a spark begin to glow within her, that spark that told her to take action. She had felt it before in her young life, and it was impossible to ignore. She had to do *something* for these hapless prisoners—but what?

Her thoughts were interrupted by a line of Unger slaves that came marching right below the spot where Kendra and her friends were hiding. They were so close that Kendra could see the lifeless expressions on their twisted faces. They were all chained together and a small black-bearded Dwarf was whipping them ahead.

"Back to yer cages, brutes!" the Dwarf bellowed. "It's time fer yer gruel!"

Then something about one of the Ungers caught Kendra's eye. "Trooogul!" she gasped out loud.

"Trooogul?" Ratchet asked. "What's that?"

"He's one of those Ungers," Kendra quickly explained. "And I know him. Trooogul is his name; he's the one I saved last year."

Ratchet let out a low whistle. Kendra stared hard at the young Unger as he marched past them, behind his fellow captives. There was no mistaking the creature. When she had first met him, Trooogul had been in serious trouble, hanging for dear life from the edge of a cliff, but Kendra could not help to think that he looked worse off now. He was burdened with heavy chains and his skin was covered in scars and bruises from the lashes of many whips. His small tusks were stained and yellow and his once-ferocious eyes were now dull and empty.

"I have to do something about this," Kendra murmured with determination. Before she knew it, she was climbing over the ledge and headed down the rocks towards the line of Unger slaves.

"Kendra, where are you going?" Ratchet exclaimed, reaching out to grab her by the cloak.

"I didn't save him for this misery," Kendra said over her shoulder, and she could feel her very face burning red. "Now let me go!"

"But there's nothing you can do for him now," Oki said.

"Just watch me," Kendra declared as she jerked away from Ratchet's grasp and slid the rest of the way down the rock ledge.

"Come on," Kendra heard Ratchet say to Oki. "We have to go with her."

The mouse let out a tiny eek, but a moment later, she heard them scrambling down the rock after her. She didn't look back, though—her eyes were focused on Trooogul and the line of Unger slaves that were now marching into the darkness ahead of her.

How did Trooogul end up here? Kendra asked herself, her mind racing.

With Ratchet and Oki close at her heels, Kendra followed the chain of Ungers out of the mine workings and down a long, dark passageway that was carved into the rock. The sounds of the mines were soon a distant clamor, but ahead she could hear the sharp crack of the Dwarven taskmaster's whip.

It was not long before they entered a large cavern. At once, Kendra realized the chamber was the site of the "pens" that had been mentioned by the Dwarf Fiddlewick, for here were many prison cells set within the rocky walls. Many of these pens were occupied, filled with all sorts of wretched looking beasts that had fallen into slavery. With a gulp, Kendra led her companions forward, deeper into the dungeon. Thankfully, the cavern was lit by only a few flickering torches, and it was easy for the three small trespassers to hide in the somber shadows.

"Look," Oki whispered with a gesture of his paw. "It's our old friend, Fiddlewick himself."

The Dwarf had been resting half-asleep on a stool at the far end of the dungeon, but now he rose to meet the Dwarven Taskmaster and his chain gang of Ungers. It was Kendra's first good look at Fiddlewick; before, she had been trying to look at him through the disguise of the cloak. Now she could see that he was holding a heavy club, and on his belt was a ring of rusted keys, which were obviously for the many cages in the dungeon.

"Eh, Druffle," Fiddlewick said to the Dwarf leading the Ungers. "You ain't seen Ornelius have ya?"

"Ain't he supposed to be here?" Druffle asked.

"He run off in them mines," Fiddlewick said. "But he's the unreliable sort anyway, I reckon."

"The king will rake his hide," Druffle said. "But I guess that's goin' to be his problem. Well, here's this lazy lot of brutes. You can get 'em fed and slumbered. They got a whole lot of minin' to do tomorrow. Hee Hee."

Kendra and her friends watched as the two Dwarves unchained Trooogul and the other Ungers and herded each of them into a cell. With this done, Druffle slung his whip over his shoulder and took his leave from the dungeon, returning (Kendra supposed) back to the mines.

"I never knew that Ungers and such smelt this bad," Ratchet commented from their hiding place. He covered his nose, for indeed, the stench was awful.

"They . . . they don't," Kendra murmured. "It's this place. It's this dirty dungeon."

There was a large cauldron bubbling in the center of the room, and now Fiddlewick began dishing out bowls of thick gray gruel for the newly-arrived slaves. With the completion of this task, the cheerful Dwarf settled himself back down on his stool.

"What now?" Oki asked.

"You two stay here," Kendra answered. "I'm going to bust Trooogul free."

"How?" Ratchet asked.

"Do you have any *Snore Galore* left?" Kendra asked. "I'm going to put Fiddlewick asleep."

"Of course," Ratchet said, handing the small pouch to her. "But do you think this is such a wise idea?"

"Trooogul won't hurt me, if that's what you mean," Kendra said firmly.

"How can you be so sure?" Oki squeaked. "He's an Unger, after all. And that's what Ungers do. They hurt Eens."

"He didn't last time," Kendra said.

"Oki's right," Ratchet said. "You can't trust those critters. Look, everyone knows that."

"Well, maybe I know something too," Kendra declared in a determined voice.

"Forget it, Ratchet," Oki said with a groan. "You won't talk her out of it now."

"Well, here, you better take my *Easy Sneeze*, too," Ratchet said, pressing a second pouch into Kendra's small hands. "It's the last of my powders, but take it, just in case. You can throw it at that fellow if he decides to take a swipe at you."

"He won't," Kendra assured the raccoon, but just to satisfy him, she took the sneezing powder anyway.

Kendra turned and crept through the shadows, towards the stool where Fiddlewick was sitting and whistling happily. As she got closer, Kendra noticed a small ridge of rock that ran up behind him. She scaled the ridge quickly, and before long, she was perched just above him. As quietly as she could, she sprinkled some of the *Snore Galore* down upon the Dwarf guard. He instantly fell asleep and Kendra quickly scrambled down to the floor. She unhooked the keys from Fiddlewick's belt before turning to face the rows of cages. She had been careful to watch which cage Trooogul had been locked up in, but it now took her a moment to scan the wall to relocate it. The pens were deep and dark, and it was not easy to see the prisoners

124

they contained. Kendra knew she had to find the right one; the last thing she wanted to do was to wander into a pen and face some unsuspecting Goojun.

After a moment, she was sure she had found Trooogul's cage, and she scampered across the floor. The prison cell was set high up in the rocks, and once again, she had to climb just to reach it. Had she had time to dwell upon her situation, she probably would have been too frightened to act, for the dungeon cells were as black as wells and the air was filled with the slurping sounds of the slaves as they devoured their gruel. But she had that spark in her now; her purpose now was not to think, but to take action.

She pulled herself up to the lip of Trooogul's cage with a grunt of effort. For a moment she rested there, on her knees, staring into the dark cave that was the Unger's prison. At first she couldn't see the creature, but after a moment she realized he was sitting in the back corner, quietly watching her. He must have heard her approach and now, even though she could only make out his faint outline in the blackness, she knew that he was watching her, waiting to see what she would do next.

"Trooogul?" she called, and she could hear the tremble in her own voice.

He didn't reply and Kendra wondered if he had heard her at all. She was just about to speak again when his voice rumbled up through the darkness, sending a shiver to the very tips of her braids.

"Youzum," he grunted. "Whozum are you?"

CHAPTER 16

K How endra
Freed the
B Beasts

If you have ever had
a chance encounter
with an old friend,
only to have him or
her stare at you blankly,
then you might know
how Kendra felt at that
moment. How could
Trooogul not remem-
ber her? She had saved
his life, only last summer,
and now he didn't even
recognize her. Kendra was
so shocked that she couldn't
even speak.

Slowly, Trooogul lumbered
out of the shadows. He walked on
all fours and looked terribly dangerous as he entered the faint light
cast by the dungeon torches. Though
he was not yet as big as the adult Ungers,
Kendra noticed he had grown since she had last
seen him—he now seemed to tower over her. Trooogul

gazed upon her with small vacant eyes, but he didn't seem to recognize her at all.

"Whozum are you?" he repeated, and there was a threatening growl to his voice.

Instinctively Kendra clutched the pouch of sneezing powder. There was a row of thick iron bars separating her and Trooogul, but she knew he could reach between them and easily seize her, if he so desired.

"Don't . . . don't you remember me?" Kendra stammered, tugging nervously at her braids.

Trooogul sat down on his haunches, like a wolf, and stared at her curiously. Their eyes locked and Kendra found herself hoping against hope that he would somehow know her. Then Trooogul's thick brow furled, as if some memory from a long-forgotten past suddenly reached him. Then, slowly, his giant mouth opened. "Youzum," he said after a moment, a hint of accusation in his voice. "Youzum little Eeneez that rescuezum Trooogul. Long time agozum, beforezum Trooogul becomezum slave."

"Yes," Kendra said, stepping forward excitedly. The bars were spaced wide enough for her to slip through, and she did, putting herself right inside the cage with the Unger.

"Whyzum comezum here?" Trooogul demanded.

"I didn't mean to," Kendra said. "We just ended up here, in these terrible mines of Umbor. But now I'm here. Now I can free you."

Trooogul snorted, though with laughter or anger, Kendra could not tell.

"Youzum! Little Eeneez!" he said. "Youzum can does nothing forzum Trooogul."

"I have these!" Kendra said, shaking the keys indignantly.

"Fatzum little Dwarfzum wearzum belt still?" Trooogul asked, scratching his claws against the rocky floor.

"Why, yes, I suppose," Kendra said. "Why? Is that how he captured you? With the belt?"

"Yeezum," Trooogul replied solemnly. "Cannot disobeyzum beltzum. Itzum magiczum! Makezum Dwarfee's wishees comes truezum."

Kendra shook her head. "We have to try anyway," she said. "The belt didn't work on us. I think it was because of Uncle Griffinskitch's own magic. His wizard staff protects us from the belt. So all we have to do is get Uncle—"

"Nozum!" Trooogul interrupted angrily. "Dwarfee catch hundredzum of Ungers with beltzum. Goojuns, Krakes and others toozum. Escape no so easyzum."

"Listen here!" Kendra said. "I can help you . . . and you can help me."

Trooogul's great brow twisted in a knot. "Howzum? Howzum Trooogul helpzum Eeneez?"

"I'm looking for something," Kendra said.

Trooogul rose back up to all fours as if in great alarm. "Whatzum?" he asked suspiciously.

"A d-door," she said, pulling anxiously on her braids again. She felt beads of perspiration rolling down her face, but she wasn't sure if it was from fear or excitement. This was her chance to discover the secret that could lead her to her family. But part of her was also afraid—for if Trooogul knew nothing of the Door to Unger, then maybe it didn't exist at all. Maybe it *was* all just a fantasy and she had led her uncle and the rest of her companions on a wild bumblebee chase.

"Doorzum?" Trooogul grunted. "What doorzum wouldzum Eeneez seek?"

"It's called the Door to Unger," Kendra said, tugging yet harder on her braids.

"Whoazum!" Trooogul exclaimed. "How does Eeneez knowzum of doorzum?"

"It exists, then?" Kendra asked excitedly. "Tell me it does!"

Trooogul sat back down on his haunches and glared at her for a moment. Then he said, "Doorzum is real. But no Eeneez shouldzum seeks doorzum."

"Why?" Kendra asked.

"Trooogul no surezum," he answered slowly. "But this muchzum Trooogul knowzum. Many Eeneez taken tozum Door to Unger. Yetzum, no Eeneez returnzum."

"But why?" Kendra urged. "Just what *is* the Door to Unger? What does it do?"

Trooogul shook his great head. "Not knowzum. Strangezum magic powerzum is at doorzum."

"You must take me there," Kendra announced.

"Nozum!" he bellowed. "Youzum blindzum? Notzum seez that Trooogul izum Unger?"

"Of course I do," Kendra said angrily. "But I'm going to set you free. I'll set all you free."

"Neverzum!" Trooogul roared ferociously. "Ungers and Eeneez enemies!"

"But last time you said that you didn't hate Eens!" Kendra cried. She felt another drop on her cheek, but it wasn't perspiration this time; it was a hot and angry tear. "Now you're saying we're enemies!"

Trooogul leaned close to her and hissed, "Of course Trooogul hate Eeneez. All Ungers hate Eeneez. Just sayzum that last timezum to make little Eeneez feel bad, to chasee awayzum."

"You're just a liar, then," Kendra said.

"And youzum," Trooogul said, spitting at her in anger, "youzum just Eeneez."

Kendra was growing desperate. She felt that Trooogul would somehow be her only chance to find her family. Somehow, she had to get him on her side. "Look," she urged, raising her hand so that he could see her palm. "I met an Unger. One of your Elders, I think. He said I was marked."

This act did not have the effect Kendra desired. For now, Trooogul's eyes went wide and he backed away from her, as if she could somehow hurt him. Even in the faint light, Kendra could see his great limbs tremble.

"You see it, don't you?" Kendra asked. "You can see the mark on my palm!"

"Itzum forbidden for any Unger to touchzum Eeneez markzee withzum star!" Trooogul uttered in a voice that was as close to a whisper as he could get.

"Why?" Kendra asked.

"Eenee with starzum will destroyzum Unger," Trooogul said, casting his eyes wildly about, as if he was looking for some desperate way to escape her presence. "Unger prophecy sayzum so. Now Eeneez must leavezum."

"Please!" Kendra urged, stepping towards him.

"NO!" Trooogul roared. "Leavezum now." And the great gray beast turned his back to her and scuttled quickly to the back of his cage.

Kendra just stood there, crying. She wondered how he could treat her so. Was this mark on her hand—a mark that she herself could not even see—so frightening? Only a moment ago, she had felt so close to discovering the next clue about the Door to Unger, a clue that could lead her to her family. But it seemed that Trooogul had dashed all her hopes just as quickly.

But Kendra had been through enough adventures to know that feeling sorry for herself wouldn't get her anywhere. With a determined yank on her braids, she composed herself. Trooogul's great bony back was still turned to her, but even so, she raised her head high and marched out of the cage and stood on the lip of the rock. Then, before she could think better of her actions, she quickly thrust one of the keys into the lock of the Unger's cage. With some luck, the very first key worked, and with a groaning creak the door swung inwards.

Trooogul whirled around, his eyes wide with surprise. "Trooogul toldzum Eeneez! Trooogul no helpzum! Whyzum Eenee setzum Trooogul freezum?"

Kendra wiped the tears from her eyes and glared at him. "Selfish beast!" she said. "You have no idea how much it cost me to save your life last time! And if you think that I did it just so you could toil the rest of your days as a slave to these greedy Dwarves, then . . . then . . . well, you truly are a monster!"

And with these words, she turned away from him and clambered down the rock. She was still holding the key ring in her hands as she turned to face the wall of cages. Her heated words had brought all the slaves scuttling to the doors of their pens, and now they clutched the bars with their gnarled claws as they glared at her. The beasts looked wild and frenzied, but Kendra's heart was now beating like a hornet's nest, and she did not care. She flung the keys as hard as she could and one of the wretched creatures reached out and greedily caught them.

"You're free!" Kendra shouted, running down the length of the dungeon. "You're all free!" Now the tears were streaming freely from her face, though she hardly understood why. She could hear a great clamor of noise; it was the doors swinging open as the keys were tossed from cage to cage, releasing slave after slave.

She stopped and turned. Creatures were now spilling out of the holes in the walls, a tidal wave of crooked limbs and wild, leering faces. Kendra gasped, for now she realized that this horde of beasts was stampeding straight toward her in their attempt to escape the dismal dungeon. She couldn't help but wonder what had become of Oki and Ratchet, but before she could quite complete this frantic thought, she heard someone yell, "STOP," and the rumbling tide of escaping slaves came to a sudden, eerie halt. Kendra stared into their faces. But they weren't looking at her, but rather *behind* her.

Slowly, the tiny Een girl turned around. There, standing on top of a large rock and glowering down upon the cavern, stood the hunched and golden-robed figure of Pugglemud.

CHAPTER 17

R King eginaldo Loses His Trousers

One might imagine Pugglemud to be quite alarmed by finding such a throng of gruesome creatures swarming, free and angry, through his dungeon. But to the contrary, he seemed quite amused by the whole affair, and now he smiled upon Kendra and the cavern full of monsters as if he knew something they did not. Then Kendra noticed that with one hand, Pugglemud was holding a large sack that seemed to wriggle and kick, and with his other, he was pulling back his cloak so that all could clearly see his magic belt.

That's why everyone obeyed his command, Kendra thought. *Pugglemud is using his belt to control us.*

Even as this occurred to her, Kendra could feel her mind growing thick and heavy. It was as if she was being locked out of her own mind; it was the power of his magic belt, and she was helpless to resist.

"Good evenin'," Pugglemud said presently. "Well, it looks like we got ourselves a—hiccup—troublemaker here!"

"Does my master still struggle with the hiccups?" Kendra asked, frowning even as the words left her mouth.

"Don't ya—hiccup—know it," the Dwarf King said. "They're a real bother. I'll have 'em for—hiccup—days, I reckon."

Just then a band of six Dwarves appeared at Pugglemud's side. Most were holding spears and swords (they were soldiers, Kendra guessed), but two of them were clutching two squirming prisoners—Ratchet and Oki!

"We found these rascals hidin' behind the rocks, King Reginaldo," one of the Dwarves reported.

"Good work," Pugglemud said, opening the sack he was holding. "We'll put 'em in with the old—hiccup—wizard and the others."

Kendra let out a gasp as her friends were dropped into the sack. "But how could you catch them?" she asked. "What about Uncle Griffinskitch's . . ."

"Ya mean this?" Pugglemud asked smugly, reaching into one of his pockets to produce Uncle Griffinskitch's wizard's staff. "Yer old uncle ain't so—hiccup—powerful without this, I reckon!"

Kendra felt her heart sink, and despite the fog that was weaving its way through her mind, everything became clear to her. Kendra knew the Dwarf king must have slipped some of his own *Snore Galore* into their dinner to put them all asleep.

Of course, Ratchet, Oki, and Kendra hadn't eaten any of the disgusting turnips, but Uncle Griffinskitch and the others certainly had. They had fallen into such a deep slumber that it had been easy for Pugglemud to sneak into their room, steal the magic staff, and capture them. He had betrayed them.

Or is it betrayal? Kendra asked herself. *He's the king. He should be able to do whatever he wants. He is, after all, my master.*

"No!" Kendra screamed out loud, clutching at her braids as if she could somehow conquer the spell. "It's your cursed belt! It's . . . it's . . ."

"Makin' ya do what I—hiccup—want, eh?" Pugglemud chortled. "Hee hee! Now that I've—hiccup—gotten yer pesky uncle and his—hiccup—magic out of the way, you can't be stoppin' the power of the—hiccup—belt, don't ya know."

He was right, Kendra knew. She felt she must obey him.

"Now what d'ya—hiccup—have to say fer yerself?" Pugglemud demanded.

"I-I-I am sorry, King Reginaldo, for my treachery," Kendra declared, kneeling before him. "Please forgive me."

"That's—hiccup—a good slave," Pugglemud said. "You'll make a fine—hiccup—slave, jus' like the—hiccup—rest of them. But how I—hiccup—wish someone could cure me of these durn hiccups!"

Kendra looked strangely at the Dwarf. In her foggy mind, so controlled by the magic belt, Kendra knew it was her duty to obey King Reginaldo's wishes. Then she thought of Ratchet's *Easy Sneeze* powder, stuffed away in her cloak. *Why, I can cure King Reginaldo's hiccups,* Kendra thought. *In fact, I must cure them, for he has wished it so.*

She reached into her cloak, found the pouch containing the powder, and approached the Dwarf king.

"Eh? Whatchya doin'?" Pugglemud asked.

"I will help you, my king," Kendra said obediently—and she cast a handful of the powder upon the Dwarf.

"What the heck is—," Pugglemud said, but before he could finish his sentence, he let out a loud "ACHOO!" It was a sneeze so strong and violent that it blew the Dwarf king right off his feet and caused him to drop Uncle Griffinskitch's staff and the sack of Een prisoners.

"How does this help?!" Pugglemud demanded, picking himself up from the ground.

"Why, your hiccups have stopped, haven't they?" Kendra asked innocently.

But before Pugglemud could muster a reply, he erupted into a fit of sneezes. Each sneeze was louder and stronger than the last, and finally, one came that was so mighty that it threw Pugglemud right against the wall of the dungeon, snapping his precious belt and causing it to fly from his fat waist and land with a dull thud upon the floor.

Instantly the fog cleared from Kendra's mind. Gone was the grip that Pugglemud's power had had upon her only seconds before. She was free!

"My pants!" Pugglemud cried, for without his belt, he had lost his trousers and now was standing in his under shorts.

In any other situation, Kendra might have laughed at Pugglemud's predicament, but now several things seemed to happen at once. The other Dwarves in the cavern all scrambled towards the magic belt and were soon ensnared in a great fistfight as each tried to get his greedy hands upon the enchanted prize. Then, there was the horde of creatures behind Kendra. All this time, they had been frozen under the spell of Pugglemud's belt, standing still as statues. But now that they were free of the Dwarf king's power they burst forward in a racket of claws and roars, all clambering over one another as they stormed to freedom. It was if a great battle had suddenly erupted in the cavern—and Kendra was right in the middle of it.

There was not a moment to lose. The first thing she had to do was get to her friends, for they were still inside the sack that was now abandoned on the floor, right in the path of the escaping monsters. Frantically, Kendra rushed towards the sack, doing her best to dodge the feet of the Goojuns, Ungers, and other terrible monsters. But before she could reach it, one of the monsters—an Unger—grabbed the sack in his crooked claw and swung it over his shoulder.

"NO!" Kendra screamed, but her cry was lost in the din of the cavern.

Then she saw her uncle's staff lying on the ground, where Pugglemud had dropped it. Quickly, she scampered towards it, but it, too, fell victim to the stampede of monsters and was crushed to splinters beneath their great bodies.

There's no magic for us now, Kendra thought, but there was no time to dwell on this sad fact. For now, she found herself in the thick of the stampede—a tiny speck amidst a sea of giants. The ground trembled underneath the pounding of so many feet and claws. It was like an earthquake and Kendra knew at any moment she would be crushed, ground to pieces, just like her uncle's staff.

Then, suddenly, Trooogul appeared before her. He was holding a strip of cloth—a ragged cloak dropped by one of the Dwarves—and now he lifted it towards her, as if he meant to cover her with it.

"What are you doing?" Kendra shrieked.

"Shutzum!" Trooogul snapped. "Don't makezum Trooogul touch Eeneez."

Being ever so careful not to touch her with his bare claws, Trooogul used the cloak to pick up Kendra. Then, using the cloak as a makeshift sack, he slung the tiny Een girl over his shoulder and charged through the underground tunnel of the Dwarves, following after his fellows.

Was Trooogul saving her? Kendra wasn't sure. She sunk down into the sack, terrified by the roar of the creatures all around her. *I have to find my friends*, she thought. But what could she do? If she leapt out of the sack, she would be crushed. And she had already seen an Unger take Uncle Griffinskitch and the others. *Maybe Trooogul will take me to them*, Kendra said to herself. *It's probably my best hope.* So she squeezed her eyes shut and sank even deeper into the sack so that she didn't have to look upon the terrible faces of the monsters that were all rushing alongside Trooogul.

The trip was a rough one. The sack bounced continuously upon Trooogul's bony back, and Kendra's body began to ache. She was desperately hungry and thirsty, but all she could do was wait. She tried screaming at Trooogul to stop so that she could rest or find something to drink, but he either didn't hear her, or just ignored her. She had no idea of their direction or how they might escape the land of Umbor. Trooogul certainly wouldn't be able to fit through the series of secret doors that Kendra had been guided through by Crumpit the day before. She assumed that Trooogul and the other creatures had discovered another way out of Umbor; after all, they had worked as slaves in the caverns and perhaps knew the place just as well as the Dwarves themselves. But if the slaves had a found a way to escape Umbor, it certainly wasn't a short one, for the horde of beasts seemed to rumble on and on through the darkness, hour after long hour. At last, Kendra blacked out and fell into a hazy nightmarish sleep.

CHAPTER 18

Trooogul Makes a Choice

When she awoke, Kendra knew at once that they had arrived at the surface of the earth. The air was fresh and strong, not at all like the stale air of Umbor. Kendra breathed in deeply. Her eyes were blurry and her head dizzy, but she could see a white slice of moon aglow in the sky. She was so happy to see it that she wished to wrap her arms around it in an embrace.

As she became better aware of her surroundings, Kendra realized that Trooogul had emptied her onto a large flat rock in a clearing of the forest. The night was quiet, especially after the pandemonium of their escape from Umbor. Kendra could see Trooogul sitting a few paces away from her. They seemed alone.

"What happened to the other creatures?" Kendra asked with sudden alarm, for they were her only link to her uncle and friends.

"No goodzum for other Ungers to seezum Trooogul withzum little Eeneez," Trooogul snorted at Kendra. "Betterzum they no knowzum Trooogul helpzum."

Kendra pulled on her braids with panic. Now what was she going to do?

"Well . . . thank you," she said to the great beast after a moment. "Thank you for saving me."

But Trooogul only grunted in reply.

"I hope that's your way of saying 'you're welcome'," Kendra said crossly. "Feel free to thank me for saving *you*."

"Never askzum Eeneez to savezum Trooogul," the Unger growled angrily.

"Why, you're just an ignorant, ungrateful beast!" Kendra retorted. "If it wasn't for me, you'd still be down there, slaving away for the Dwarves!"

Trooogul's nostrils flared with rage, and Kendra wondered for a moment if she had pressed her luck too far. Trooogul was much bigger than she was, and she knew the Unger could easily crush her—if he so wished. But he did not crush her. Instead he said, "Unger Law sayzum all Eeneez gozum to Door to Unger."

"Good," Kendra announced. "That's exactly where I need to go."

Trooogul paced back and forth in front of her, snorting. Kendra could see that the creature was in deep thought, but only after a few moments did he say, "Youzum! Youzum no gozum door!"

"Why?" Kendra asked.

"No gozum door!" Trooogul barked again. "Youzum have-zum forbidden mark. Prophecy sayzum Eenee with mark no gozum to Doorzum."

"So what do you plan to do?" Kendra demanded impatiently.

"Unger law sayzum if Eeneez no go to door, then Eeneez die," Trooogul said, as quietly as he could.

"What are you talking about?" Kendra asked furiously. "You're going to kill me? I just saved your sorry rump! I'm going to have to stop helping you out if this is how you plan to repay me!"

"No needzum Eeneez help!" Trooogul yelled.

"Then stop getting into trouble!" Kendra shouted back.

Trooogul snorted again then sat down on his haunches and stared at her, fuming in silence. Kendra could see that he was trying to decide what to do.

Would he really kill me after everything we've been through? Kendra asked herself. She wondered if she should make a run for it; but her legs were still numb from the long journey in the sack. She would never be able to escape the great beast. So she sat there staring back at him quietly.

But the silence was not to last. A ruckus came from the trees and they both turned in the direction of the sound.

"Beasties comezum," Trooogul said.

"Who?" Kendra asked in a whisper.

Then, as if to answer her question, the foliage parted and a trio of Ungers appeared in the little clearing.

"Itzum Trooogul's friendzums," Trooogul murmured with a grimace.

Kendra could see by the look of the Ungers that they had been among the slaves who had escaped from Umbor, for they were quite thin and gray—just like Trooogul. They also seemed about the same age and size as Trooogul, so she supposed that is why they were friends. Then Kendra spotted a sack slung over one of the Unger's shoulders.

"It's Uncle Griffinskitch and the others!" Kendra gasped, but before she could dwell upon this happy turn of events, the Unger carrying the sack spoke.

"Lookzum, Trooogul!" the creature chortled.

He held up the sack and jiggled it, and it moved in response. Her friends were still alive, at least, but Kendra knew there would be no way for them to escape without her help. Jinx, as strong as she was, didn't have her weapons. Uncle Griffinskitch's staff was destroyed, and even Ratchet had used up all his powders. It was up to her to save them.

"Creeegun capturezum whole gang of Eeneez," the Unger with the sack continued, speaking directly to Trooogul. "Youzum catchum only onezum? Hee hee. Beezum careful letting itzum runzee around loosezum. Little Eeneez quickzum; might runnzum awayzum."

Trooogul eyed the Unger called Creeegun carefully and after a moment said, "No carezum. Trooogul letting Eeneez go freezum."

"What?" Kendra cried, peering from behind Trooogul's great body. "Just a minute ago you said—,"

"Eeneez shutzum mouth!" Trooogul bellowed, turning back to snap at her.

"Whatzum Trooogul talking aboutzum!?" Creeegun cried. "Youzum go crazyies?! Wezum must takezum Eeneez to doorzum!"

"Nozum!" Trooogul said, the hair on his back bristling as he paced back and forth in front of Creeegun and the other Ungers. "Eeneez savezum beasties. Shouldzum go freezum!"

"But I want to go to the D—," Kendra tried to say.

"Shutzum!" Trooogul yelled, looking back at her with rage in his eyes.

"Whatzum wrong with Trooogul?" Creeegun asked, pointing a crooked claw at him. "Youzum! Youzum should no helpzum Eeneez. Ungers and Eeneez enemies."

"Then whyzum Eeneez helpzum Ungers?" Trooogul demanded. "Eeneez no enemy."

"Itzum Eeneez trickzum," Creeegun replied.

"NOZUM!" Trooogul shouted.

The outrage in his voice startled Kendra. Her mind was swimming with confusion. One minute Trooogul was saying that it was his duty to kill her—and the next minute he was trying to protect her. She sensed a great battle waging inside of Trooogul. He was struggling with what to do. Kendra only hoped that his choice would end up in her favor.

Then Trooogul said to Creeegun, "If not for Eeneez, Ungers still be slavezum to Dwarfee. Izum that no worthzum Eenee lifezum?"

"No Eeneez shouldzum be sparedzum," Creeegun decreed loudly. "Unger law sayzum *all* Eeneez be taken to Doorzum to Unger."

"Not this onezum," Trooogul snarled in reply, and he stared hard at Creeegun and the other Ungers.

"Trooogul alwayzum strange Unger," Creeegun declared. "But thizum wrong, to takezum side of Eeneez against Ungers. Youzum! Youzum shouldzum come with Creeegun. Wezum takezum Eeneez to Door to Unger! Togetherzum becomezee heroes!"

But Trooogul did not falter. He stood firm before Creeegun and the other Ungers, like a statue. For a tense moment, no one said a thing, and all Kendra could hear was the deep, snorting breaths of the creatures. She could see Creeegun's eyes burn with hatred in the moonlight. It seemed to her that he might leap upon Trooogul and attack at any moment.

Then, suddenly, Creeegun said, "If Trooogul no takezum Eeneez, then Creeegun willzum!" And with this, the great beast reached toward Kendra with one of his crooked claws.

With a shriek, Kendra threw her hands up in front of her, as if it would somehow protect her—and, strangely, it did. For at that moment, the moonlight caught the hidden star upon her palm and at once, Creeegun and his fellow Ungers gasped in horror. The Ungers all stepped back and immediately broke into frantic speech.

"The forbiddens Eeneez!"

"Killz it!"

"Nozum! Don't even touchzum!"

Creeegun stared at Trooogul with terrified eyes. "You-zum!" he cried. "Youzum protectzum forbidden Eeneez! The onezum who wouldzum destroyzum Unger!"

Trooogul said nothing; he just sat there, frozen.

"Traitor!" Creeegun yelled. He leaned forward and struck Trooogul so hard that the young Unger toppled backward with a startled cry of pain. Then, shouldering the sack, Creee-gun and the other Ungers tore off into the night without even so much as another look in Kendra's direction.

Kendra could hardly believe it. Everything had happened so quickly. She peered over the edge of the rock and looked at Trooogul. He was in a crumpled heap on the ground.

"Trooogul," she said quietly. "Are you okay?"

He looked up at her, his beady eyes fraught with pain and anger. But he said nothing.

"Why didn't they kill me?" Kendra asked.

"Little Eeneez frightenzum Ungers," Trooogul replied after a moment. "Creeegun afraidzum of Eeneez curse. Safer to run-zum away. Eeneez with mark must no gozum to doorzum."

"Well, then your friends are in for a surprise," Kendra declared. "I'm going after my uncle and the others. I'm going to the door."

"Foolzum!" Trooogul snarled, leaping up to the rock with such quickness that Kendra jumped in fear. "Trooogul just savedzum lifezum of Eeneez!"

"Good!" Kendra retorted. "We're almost even then."

"Little foolzum not so luckyzum next timezum," Trooogul snarled. "Maybezum Ungers killzum Eeneez. And Trooogul no be therezum."

"Why?" Kendra asked him anxiously. "What are you going to do?"

Trooogul shrugged and turned his back on her. "No know-zum. Now Trooogul shunned by Ungers. Creeegun will spread wordzum of Trooogul. Trooogul becomezum outcast."

"Then come with me," Kendra urged.

"Nozum!" Trooogul growled, whirling around to glare at her. "Youzum! Youzum worst thingzum ever happens to Trooogul! Allzum little Eeneez dozum is bringzum troubles to Trooogul."

"Trouble!" Kendra cried indignantly. "Then why do I always seem to save your sorry backside?"

Her words infuriated Trooogul. He leaned forward and roared so loud that it knocked Kendra off her feet. Then, with an angry snort, he leapt down from the rock and scampered into the forest, in the opposite direction from where the other Ungers had gone. Kendra pulled herself up by the elbows and quietly watched his silhouette melt into the darkness.

Now I'm truly alone, she said to herself in the now-quiet night.

CHAPTER 19

The Hunters
in the Forest

Kendra

was not sure how long she remained lying on the rock, staring up at the night sky. *Soon, it will be the first moon of summer,* Kendra thought. *Then it will be too late to find the Door—at least according to what the Unger Oroook said.*

But she needed to find it, she reminded herself—and now more than ever. Her uncle and the others were being taken to the door—and it was all because of her. She was the reason they were on this journey and now if she didn't find them—well, who knew what would become of them?

Many thoughts swirled through Kendra's mind. So much had happened in a short time, and the mystery of her past was beginning to unravel. Now she understood why the Ungers had not taken her as a baby. They had captured the rest of her family—but when they had seen her mark, they must have become frightened and decided to leave her behind to die in the wilderness. She hadn't died, of course; Uncle Griffinskitch had found her and looked after her.

But he won't find me this time, Kendra thought. *Because now it's all happened again and this time the Ungers have captured Uncle Griffinskitch and everyone else. Everyone except me, of course. And it's all because of this stupid mark!*

She studied her hand for the hundredth time, hoping somehow that she could see the mark that kept sparing her from capture. She could not, of course, and in her anger, she smacked her hand against the rock.

If it wasn't for this ridiculous mark, I'd be with Uncle Griffinskitch, and Oki, and Ratchet, and everyone else right now, she thought.

Kendra was not sure how long she sat there in solitude. At last hunger and thirst got the better of her and she rose to go forage in the woods. She was a tiny creature in an enormous place, but there is sometimes a great advantage to being so small, for sometimes a little will do a lot. A few drops from a shallow puddle satisfied Kendra's thirst, while a seed here and a berry there filled her tummy. Thus refreshed, she found a tiny space in the nook of a tree root and curled up to go to sleep. It was a fitful rest in a strange place, but it was far better then being bounced around in a sack. She was not sure what tomorrow would bring—but she was determined to find and rescue her companions.

For the next several days, Kendra followed the trail that Creeegun and his friends had cut through the forest. The beasts' footprints were huge and easy to follow, and Kendra knew they would eventually lead her to the Door to Unger. That was, of course, if she survived the journey. For now that she was alone, the world seemed more frightening than she could have ever imagined. The forest creaked and groaned with strange noises, and menacing animals seemed to prowl around every corner. These were wild things, nothing like the animals back in the land of Een. Kendra had traveled in the wilderness before, of course, in her search for the Box of Whispers—but on that journey, she had been shielded from such creatures by Uncle Griffinskitch's magic. Now she was without his protection, and Kendra wondered if she could ever reach the Door to Unger without it.

I have to, she told herself. *Uncle Griffinskitch, Oki—and everyone—are all depending on me.*

Sometimes she wondered what had become of Trooogul. She was thankful that he had saved her, but when she remembered his last words to her, they still stung. "You're the worst thing that ever happened to me," he had said. Well, it wasn't quite like that, for he had said it in his Unger voice.

I wonder when I'll see him again? she wondered to herself. *Probably never.*

But she did encounter the young Unger, and it was only a few days later. She was taking a drink at a quiet stream in the woods when he suddenly appeared at the opposite bank. He seemed just as surprised to see her and cast an angry scowl in her direction.

"What's your problem?" Kendra demanded. "Do you own this stream?"

Trooogul grunted at her and dipped his claw into the water for a drink.

Kendra gave her braids a pull. "Maybe you're just following me."

"Thatzum nonsense!" Trooogul snarled. "Trooogul despizum little Eeneez."

"Good," Kendra retorted childishly. "I despise you too."

"Little Eeneez nothing but badzum luck!" the Unger growled.

"You seem to run into quite enough bad luck without my help," Kendra returned. "That's why you always need me to rescue you."

Trooogul looked as if he was about to explode in anger, but just then there was a *whoosh*, and a spear suddenly cut through the air and shot right through Kendra's cloak, pinning her to the ground.

The spear had come from behind her. With some difficulty, Kendra strained her head back, only to discover a half-dozen of some of the most surprising creatures she had ever seen running through the brush towards her. The creatures were quite tall, and, at first, Kendra thought that they must be giants, for while she had never met one in person, she had seen pictures of them in Professor Bumblebean's books. But those books had depicted giants as big, burly beasts, and these creatures were rather slender. Indeed, Kendra decided that they looked rather like oversized Eens, except they wore no braids and their ears were round instead of pointed.

Then one of the creatures spoke.

"Hurry!" it shouted. "These Elves are slippery folk!"

"It'll catch a fair piece of gold, that's for sure!" another added.

Now these words would have sounded normal to someone like you or me; but to Kendra, who spoke the language of Eens, the creatures' speech was strange and garbled. What she did understand, however, was the fact that one of the creatures had thrown a spear at her, and that's all she needed to know that she was in grave trouble. She tugged on the spear with both hands, but when she couldn't dislodge it from the ground she frantically began pulling on her cloak.

"Come on!" she cried, but even though her cloak began to rip, she could not pull free from the spear. She could hear the hunters; at any moment they would be upon her.

Then, suddenly, Trooogul was there. In what seemed like a single motion, he leapt across the stream, wrenched Kendra free of the spear, and lifted her up in one of his mighty claws.

"You let me go!" Kendra shouted angrily, despite how frightened she was. "I thought I was cursed!"

"Shutzum!" Trooogul hissed, his rocky face only inches away from Kendra's. "Youzum no wantzum be captured!"

His tone so frightened Kendra that she immediately threw her arms around his thick neck.

"Why?" Kendra gasped. "What are they?"

"Humanz!" Trooogul snorted in reply as he turned and scaled the nearest tree. With a long bony claw he grabbed

hold of one of the many vines hanging down from the tree's limbs and swung towards the next tree.

"Hey!" Kendra heard one of the humans shout. "That Troll just stole our Elf! C'mon, we got to get them!"

Even though Kendra could not see them, she knew the humans were coming in pursuit, for they were making a tremendous racket—shouting and cursing as they crashed through the forest. It was up to Trooogul now to save them. As their vine reached the end of its arc, the Unger reached out with his claw to grab another dangling vine, and they were once again on the swing. In this way, they began to swoop through the forest, vine by vine. For Kendra, the world soon became a whirl of lush greens and patches of turquoise sky. She squeezed her eyes shut, trying to block out the feeling in her stomach.

She had never experienced such a dizzying trip, yet even through it, one thing pushed to the front of her mind: Trooogul had allowed himself to touch her.

"Th-thank you," Kendra stammered, clutching Trooogul's skin with all her might.

"Whatzum for?" Trooogul grunted, reaching for another vine with one of his great claws.

"You saved me," Kendra murmured.

"No safezum yet," Trooogul retorted. "Besidezum . . . what choicezum Trooogul havezum? Someonezum mustz rescuezum Eenee. Youzum goodz at findingzum trouble."

"Ha ha," Kendra said. "You're almost as funny as you look."

Trooogul grunted, and it was the type of sound that made Kendra think of one of Uncle Griffinskitch's humphs. "Maybe Trooogul just dropzum Eenee," the Unger said.

But he didn't have to make good on this threat; for in the next moment, one of the humans hurled a spear through the forest and it sliced through the vine that Trooogul was holding. Kendra clung tightly to the great Unger as he plummeted down through the trees, hitting and snapping branches as he dropped. The branches helped to break their fall, but they still crashed to the ground with such force that they were sent sprawling in different directions.

It took Kendra a moment to pull herself up to her elbows. She groaned and rubbed her head. Though her ears were ringing, she could hear the whoops and hollers of the humans as they charged through the forest toward them. Kendra cast her eyes about wildly. They had landed in a small clearing, at the shore of a lagoon, but it seemed that there was no good place to hide.

As for Trooogul, he had already risen to all fours and was now pacing nervously about the clearing, sniffing at the air with a curious expression on his face. He was scratched and torn from his fall, but if he was in pain, he did not show it. On the contrary, Kendra could see the great beast's mind at work. His brow furled as if he were trying to remember something. He picked up a broken branch and dipped it into the waters of the lagoon.

"What is it?" Kendra asked anxiously, joining him by the shore. The sounds of the humans were louder now; they would be upon them in an instant.

Trooogul's eyes suddenly went wide with astonishment. "Cavezum!" he cried.

"What are you talking about?" Kendra gasped.

"Holdzum breath!" Trooogul bellowed—and with that, he snatched Kendra close to his chest and plunged headlong into the water.

CHAPTER 20

A Clue for Kendra

We all know that there is nothing that can prepare one for the sudden chill of water when you dive into a lake or river. Thinking about it first never helps, but thankfully for Kendra, she hadn't been given the time to think. One minute she was standing at the lagoon's edge with Trooogul, and the next, he had grabbed her and leapt into the cold murky water.

As soon as she hit the water, it was as if all of Kendra's senses were suddenly shut off. Instantly her whole body went numb with shock and the world went dark. The shouts of the hunters became muffled before they faded away all together. Trooogul's arms grasped the Een girl tightly, and she could feel the water swirl around them as the Unger kicked his strong legs, propelling them forward along the bottom of the lagoon. Kendra felt as if her lungs would burst. How long would she be able to hold her breath?

Then, the next thing Kendra knew, she was lying on a floor of rock, panting heavily as the water dripped from her body. It was so dark that she couldn't see a thing.

"Where are we?" she gasped, trying to catch her breath. Her voice echoed.

"Thiszum secret cavezum," Trooogul said, though she couldn't see him in the darkness. "Hiddens beneathzum water. Safe nowzum. Humans no findzum Trooogul and Eenee."

"How can you be so sure?" Kendra asked between chattering teeth.

"Humans lazy creatures," the Unger said. "Soon givezum up chase."

"It's pitch black in here," Kendra said.

"Waitzum," Trooogul said, and Kendra could hear him rummaging around in the darkness.

"What are you doing?" she asked.

"Therezum supplies herezum," the Unger replied. "Trooogul findzum torchee."

"I guess we're not the first ones to use this place," Kendra remarked.

A moment later, the cave became aglow with a faint light, and Kendra could see Trooogul holding a stick of burning wood. She also noticed that he had a large gash in one of his arms—he had obviously been hurt during their fall to the forest floor.

"You're bleeding," Kendra said. "Here, let me look at you."

She reached for the great Unger, but he pulled away, nervously.

"What?" Kendra asked. "It's not this curse nonsense, is it? You just carried me halfway across the forest! I think you would have shriveled up by now if my touch was so cursed."

Trooogul grunted.

"I guess you'll just have to learn to trust me," Kendra said.

Trooogul glared at her and at last sat back on his haunches to let Kendra attend to his injury. The Een girl searched through the small store of supplies where Trooogul had found the torch and soon produced a few strips of cloth that she could use to make a bandage.

"No tiezum bandage too tightzum," Trooogul grumbled as Kendra dressed his wound.

"Don't be such a baby," Kendra said.

"Eeneez speakzum too muchzum," Trooogul retorted. "Maybe Trooogul no despizum Eeneez so much if Eeneez just shutzum mouthzum."

"Well, you're an Unger and I'm an Een," Kendra remarked mockingly. "We're supposed to hate each other."

Trooogul grunted again.

"You do sound just like my Uncle Griffinskitch," Kendra returned. Despite the fact that she was cold and wet (and still trembling from their escape from the humans), she suddenly found herself cheering up. Maybe it was because she knew she was no longer alone. "How did you know this place was here?" Kendra asked as she finished with Trooogul's repairs. "You must have been here before."

"Trooogul no rememberzum coming to cavezum," the Unger replied. "Cannot explainzum. Maybezum herezum long agozum...whenzum just Ungerling."

"But why?" Kendra persisted.

Trooogul shook his head, clearly quite confused. "No knowzum. Itzum likezum . . . likezum dream."

"Lucky for us, in any case," Kendra declared. "Well, come on. Let's explore this cave; maybe we can find a way out of here."

As she moved, her foot happened to brush against something on the ground that made a sharp clink. "What was that?" she wondered.

Trooogul held the torch to the rocky floor and there they saw a tiny round metal object. Kendra stooped to pick it up.

"It looks like a pocket watch," Kendra remarked, raising it to the light. "And it's small, like an Een-sized gadget. But what would it be doing *here*?"

"Openz it," Trooogul suggested.

The object was tarnished and rusty, and it took Kendra a moment to make the clasp release—but when it did she let out a cry.

"Whatzum?!" Trooogul asked.

"It . . . it's a compass," Kendra stammered. "There's an inscription: *'To Kiro, on your fifth birthday, so you won't get lost. From Uncle Griffinskitch'.*"

Trooogul looked at her, puzzled, but for a moment Kendra couldn't speak. Her mind was a jumble of thoughts and emotions. This entire journey had been based on nothing more than a strange story given to her by an Unger in the middle of the night. But now, at last, she had a real clue about her family. The compass was something she could touch, something she could hold. It proved that her family—or her brother, at least—had been in this very cave. It meant she was on the right track.

"This . . . this was my brother's," Kendra finally told Trooogul.

"Brotherzum?" the Unger asked incredulously.

"Y-yes," Kendra uttered. "Uncle Griffinskitch must have given it to Kiro before he and my parents disappeared. But . . . but . . . how did it come to be in this wretched cave?"

"Eenee's brother mustzum have been in this cavezum, many moonzum ago," Trooogul said, staring at the compass. "Maybe Eenee's brother dropzum compass herezum."

Kendra glared at the great beast. "Did you know him?!" she demanded angrily.

"Youzum brother?" Trooogul cried. "How Trooogul knowzum brother?"

"You knew this cave was here!" Kendra said in an accusatory tone. "How? You must have been here before, all those years ago! You were with the Ungers that captured my family and took them to the door!"

"Eeneez talking crazies," Trooogul retorted. "Trooogul say no rememberzum being here! Maybe little Eeneez should cleaneez earzum!"

"Then how did you know this cave was here?" Kendra asked, jabbing a finger at him. "You're not telling me something."

"Trooogul tellzum everything Trooogul knowzum!"

"I don't believe you!" Kendra insisted.

"Trooogul no carezum!" Trooogul barked. "If Trooogul takezum family, why savezum little Eeneez now? Why helpzum?"

Kendra sat there, glowering at him. By the flicker of the torchlight, he looked to her more terrifying and horrific then he ever had before. Somehow, he knew what had happened to her family. He *had* to.

"Trooogul tellzum truth," Trooogul said after a moment. "Maybezum needzum trust Trooogul."

Kendra felt a tear run down her cheek. She ran her fingers over the words etched inside the compass. In so many ways, the tiny compass was the closest connection she had ever had with her brother. Uncle Griffinskitch had always told her so little about her family. Now here in front of her was a piece of Kiro, a piece of her family. She imagined Kiro receiving the gift from her uncle. She imagined her brother as a small boy, holding the compass in his hands, just as she was now.

"You don't understand," she murmured, turning to look back at Trooogul. "You don't know what it's like to not have a family."

"How doezum little Eeneez know howzum Trooogul feel?" the Unger snapped, rising to all fours. "Youzum! Youzum know nothingzum of Trooogul. Trooogul havezum no clanzum!"

"Why?" she asked, trembling as she spoke. "What happened to your clan?"

Trooogul glared at her. "Unger Elders sayzum Eeneez kill Trooogul's clanzum when Trooogul just Ungerling."

164

"That's impossible!" Kendra cried.

Trooogul let out an angry snort. "Maybe little Eeneez own family killzum Trooogul's clanzum! Youzum ever think-zum that?"

"That can't be!" Kendra said. "You're twisting things!"

"Stupid little Eeneez," Trooogul huffed, backing off into the dark shadows of the cavern. "Youzum! Youzum think knowzum everythings."

Kendra watched the large monster disappear into the darkness. He extinguished the torch and the cave was cast back into utter darkness. Kendra pulled her wet cloak tight against her body and just sat there as her mind swelled with a thousand thoughts. *Can I trust Trooogul? Does he truly know nothing of my brother? Or is he lying? Does he know exactly what became of him and is just tricking me now, to lead me to the same fate?*

Maybe I should just leave behind the wretched cave and take my chances with the humans, she thought, tugging fretfully on her braids. But she couldn't make her legs move. After a while she began to hear the loud snores of Trooogul from the other side of the dark cave. If she was to escape, now would be the time. Then again, Trooogul could be the only link to her brother, maybe to her entire family. *What should I do?* Kendra asked herself. This question coursed through her mind, but before she could quite find an answer to it, she slipped into a deep sleep, her hand clenched tightly around her brother's compass.

CHAPTER 21

A pair of Unlikely Companions

When Kendra awoke many hours later a small fire was burning in the center of the cave and there was a branch of wild berries resting next to her. Trooogul was awake, sitting near the fire and watching her.

With a nervous tug of her braids, Kendra sat up and returned his gaze.

"Where did the berries come from?" Kendra asked.

"Trooogul go outzum already," the Unger said. "Getzum breakfast forzum Eenee."

"Th-thank you," Kendra said. She tucked her brother's compass into her pouch and moved closer to the warm fire to nibble on the berries.

167

For a while they sat in silence. Then Kendra asked, "Do you know anything about your family?"

"Nozum," came the gruff reply.

"You have no memory of them at all?" she asked.

"Nozum," the Unger repeated. "After meetzum little Eeenee last year, Trooogul beginzum asking Elders questions aboutzum land of Eeneez. Elders tell Trooogul thatzum Eeneez killzum Trooogul's clan."

"It just can't be," Kendra murmured.

"It nozum matter," Trooogul said. "Trooogul clanzum dead. Thatzum all that matterzum."

"You're an orphan, just like me," Kendra said quietly.

"Nozum," Trooogul said. "Youzum have clan stillzum; Eeneez havezum Uncle."

"Yes," Kendra said. "But just like you, I have no memory of my mother or father—or my brother. And now Uncle Griffinskitch is gone too."

"Trooogul go with little Eeneez to Doorzum to Unger," Trooogul announced abruptly.

"What?" Kendra cried in surprise. "Why?"

"Trooogul mustzum," the great creature said. "Whole lifezum, Trooogul knowzum nothing aboutzum clan. Now Trooogul's friends shuns him too. Trooogul havezum nothing. No friendzum. No clanzum. Many questions Trooogul havezum. Just likezum Eeneez."

Kendra fiddled with her braids, deep in thought. The most important thing, she knew, was to find the Door to Unger. Being chased by the humans had meant she had lost Creeegun's trail through the forest—now, if she was to find the door, she knew she'd probably need to trust Trooogul. That, of course, was the hard part.

"Did you know Oroook?" Kendra asked Trooogul. "The Unger who came to see me in Een?"

Trooogul shook his head. "Nozum. But many Unger no likezum Oroook."

"Why?" Kendra asked.

"Sayzum Oroook have strangezum ideas," Trooogul replied.

"And what do you think?" Kendra asked.

"No knowzum anythingzum anymore," Trooogul said, casting his dull eyes to the ground.

"Oroook said the door is located in the Greeven Wastes," Kendra said. "Is that true?"

"Yeezum," Trooogul replied. "What elsezum Oroook sayzum?"

"That he knew my mother," Kendra replied. "And that the Door to Unger would be the key to finding her and my family. He said it was the door to truth."

"Then we mustzum finds it," Trooogul said gravely.

For the next week Kendra and the great beast trekked northward, towards the Greeven Wastes. They did not know the exact way, for Trooogul himself had never been there (or so he said), but he did seem to have a sense of the general direction.

It was during these days of weary travel that Kendra came to learn more about Trooogul and the way of Ungers. At first the beast was not inclined to speak to Kendra any more than he had to, but she chattered at him so much that he eventually softened and started to speak about his life. He explained how he had been raised by the Elders in his village and that he had no memory of his real family. He also told Kendra about the day he, Creeegun, and a few of his other friends had been captured by the Dwarves. They had been swimming in a lagoon near the Hills of Horm when Pugglemud had suddenly appeared with his belt and commanded them to follow him. Of course, they could not resist the magic of the belt and were led straight into the dreadful mines of Umbor. That had been months ago—and he had been a slave ever since, up to the moment when Kendra had rescued him.

There were a few things that Kendra didn't want to know about Ungers. For instance, she was terrified to know what Trooogul ate. Kendra herself existed off seeds, berries, and nuts, but the Unger rarely partook of these things. She knew that Trooogul disappeared for a few hours each night after she had fallen asleep and she assumed it was during these times that he filled his belly.

Then finally, her curiosity got the better of her. One night after he returned, Kendra asked, "Where have you been?"

"Wherezum Eenee thinkzum?" he grunted. "Trooogul gozum hunting."

"That's horrible!" Kendra said. "What do you hunt for?"

"Little creatures," the Unger replied.

"How can you?" Kendra cried. "They're my friends!"

"No eatzum Eenee critters!" Trooogul returned. "You thinkzum Trooogul some sortzum monster? Only eatzum dummee animalzum."

"Dumb animals?" Kendra asked. "What do you mean?"

"How comezum Eenee no knowzum difference?" Trooogul asked impatiently. "Eenee critters canzum talk. Canzum do thingzum other animalzum no dozum. Itzum because of magic in landzum of Eeneez."

Kendra twirled one of her braids around a finger as she tried to recall her history lessons from school. She had learned that the magic of Een had changed the animals inside her enchanted land over hundreds and hundreds of years, so that they were different from the animals of the outside world. What she had never known was *how* they were different.

"Itzum crimezum for Unger to eatzum any intelligentee critter," Trooogul explained.

"A crime?" Kendra asked incredulously. "I would have thought Ungers would eat anything."

"That's becauzum youzum Eeneez," Trooogul snorted. "And Eeneez thinkzum knowzum everything."

"You know, you could be a whole lot kinder," Kendra told the beast.

"Trooogul no kindzum to annoying littlezum Eeneez that he despizum," came the reply.

"Fine," Kendra said. "Just so you know, I don't like you very much either. Especially right now."

"Goodzee," Trooogul uttered. "Thatzum way supposed to be betweenzum Unger and Eeneez."

Kendra threw her hands into air. "FINE," she said. "Be that way."

171

As it turned out, there was less and less eating for both of them in the following days. For now the landscape began to change. The forests thinned, and soon the only trees were thin and short, with brown and brittle leaves. The bushes turned gray and drooped over as if thirsting for water, of which there seemed to be very little. There were very few berries or seeds, and scarcely a critter to be found amidst the failing countryside.

If she had not known better, Kendra would have thought winter was arriving. Then she remembered the words from the *Legend of the Wizard Greeve*: " . . . and in that place the plants withered, the rivers shrank, and the great trees fell."

"We must be getting close," Kendra told Trooogul. "This place is dark and desolate—just like the Greeven Wastes are said to be."

The nights became colder. Trooogul thought a fire would not be a good idea, so most times Kendra shivered herself to sleep. Then, one night, she awoke to the sound of her own teeth chattering.

"I'm freezing!" she moaned.

She looked over at Trooogul, hunched over and sleeping soundly. He looked like a great boulder. Slowly she crept over to his big body and touched him. How warm he was! She gave her braids a nervous yank. Traveling with the Unger was one thing; curling up next to him was another. But she was too cold to dwell on the idea, so she quickly nestled against his thick gray body.

"Whatzum doing?" Trooogul murmured, stirring from his slumber.

"I'm freezing," Kendra told him.

Trooogul opened one large, sleepy eye and gave her an inquisitive look.

"Really freezing," Kendra said.

"Okayzum, Little Star," he muttered groggily.

"What did you call me?" Kendra asked.

"Hmm? Whatzum?" Trooogul grunted.

"You called me 'Little Star'," Kendra told him. "It was almost kind."

"Trooogul half-asleepzum!" the Unger grunted angrily. "Little Eenee shouldzum shutzum and go sleepzee toozum."

Kendra shrugged and snuggled in close to Trooogul. She felt the coldness melt from her body and happily, she sighed. That night she had her best sleep in a week.

CHAPTER 22

The Strange Song and Who Sang It

The next morning, before the dull sun had quite managed to gleam upon the somber landscape, Kendra was awoken by a strange voice weaving through the lonely trees. The tiny girl arose and rubbed her eyes, at first thinking that she must be dreaming. Then she heard the voice again. It came as a song, and Kendra heard these words:

> *If you have a griffin in the closet*
> *Why you just can't toss it*
> *But don't be so forlorn*
> *Just call for Effryn Hagglehorn.*

"How strange," Kendra remarked. Trooogul was still sound asleep, so she shook the great beast awake. "Listen," she said. "Can you hear this song?"

Trooogul cocked his ear to the sound and listened to the next verse. "Soundzum like somethingee dying," he said after a moment.

"It sounds like a happy sort of song, if you ask me," Kendra said.

They listened again:

If you have a boil on your bottom,
Well, that's pretty rotten
But don't prick it with a thorn
Just ask for Effryn Hagglehorn!

"Thatzum no happyzum song," Trooogul declared. "Bottoms and boilzums!"

"Come on!" Kendra urged. "Let's go meet this singer."

"Trooogul thought Eeneez supposed to be scaredzum of everythingzum," Trooogul snorted.

"That's the problem with Ungers," Kendra laughed as she darted off through the scrub towards the voice. "They think they know everything."

The sun was now beginning to light the way, and in another moment, the two companions came upon a curious scene. Here, in a hollow in the bushes, was an odd-looking fellow, hanging upside down from a sort of snare attached to a small tree that was bowing slightly over with his weight. The creature had been caught by his feet (or hooves, rather, Kendra realized), but he did not appear the least bit worried about his predicament; indeed, if anything, he seemed rather amused.

Kendra studied the droll fellow with an inquisitive tug of her braids. He was about the size of a Dwarf, but that was about where the similarity ended. The entire bottom-half of the creature was covered in fur and not only did he have hooves, but also a tail with a bushy end, like a paintbrush. His top half was quite different, for he wore no cloak or shirt and Kendra could plainly see his round little belly, which seemed to jiggle as he hung above her. As for his face, he had a long beard, two large ears that stuck out at right angles, and twinkling green eyes that were roofed by curly eyebrows. On the very top of his head were two horns that coiled forward like a pair of hooks.

"Why, I know what you are!" Kendra exclaimed after a moment. "You're a Faun! We have a statue of one right in the middle of Faun's End."

"Well shave my shins!" the creature said as he regarded Kendra. "You must be an Een, if you know Faun's End."

"Of course I'm an Een," Kendra said.

"A pleasure to meet you," the Faun said, extending one of his chubby hands for Kendra to shake, though he was far too high up for her to reach. When he realized this gesture was in vain, the Faun turned his attention to Trooogul and said, "Well, clip my crown! It's an Unger of all things, rubbing elbows with an Een. Aren't you two supposed to be mortal enemies?"

"Yeezum," Trooogul muttered grumpily, sitting down in front of the dangling Faun.

"We've called a truce," Kendra explained. "But Mr. Faun—or, er—I don't know what to call you—how did you end up hanging here?"

"Butter my beard!" the Faun exclaimed, swaying in the air as he spoke. "Imagine my manners at not introducing myself properly. Why, I'm Effryn, Effryn Hagglehorn to be exact, purveyor of magical goods. Cures, charms, and curios—all things enchanted, if you will. If you have any problems, well, then I'm your Faun."

"I'm Kendra," the Een girl said. "And this is Trooogul. But it seems to me that you're the one who has a problem right now. Do you need us to rescue you?"

"Why, not at all!" Effryn said cheerfully.

"But little Eeneez likezum playing rescue," Trooogul grumbled.

"Oh shut it," Kendra said to the Unger. "If it wasn't for me you'd be dangling off some cliff or breaking rocks for Pugglemud!"

"Annoying little Eeneez," the Unger sneered.

"Oh, my!" Effryn bleated. "You two argue just like my children—well, if I had any children, which I don't. But if I did, I'm sure they'd argue just like you."

Trooogul grunted and said, "Why little Faunee not usee magic to getzum out of trapzum?"

"Why, I was just getting to that," Effryn proclaimed. "Then you two came along and completely interrupted my plan."

"Er . . . and what plan is that?" Kendra asked skeptically.

"Well, it involves a bit of patience," Effryn admitted. "Mostly because Skeezle is so slow. But he'll get to me soon enough."

"Skeezle?" Trooogul asked, casting his eyes about, as if he expected someone (or something) to appear at any moment.

"Where is this . . . Skeezle?" Kendra asked.

"Oh, he's been here the whole time," Effryn said. "You just haven't seen him. He's making his way up the trunk of this pesky tree, which some cruel creature has used to ensnare me."

Kendra took a step closer to the tree, but the only thing she saw was a tiny snail, making the long and tediously slow journey up the trunk. Then, upon second look, Kendra saw that a miniature box was strapped to the back of the little creature. There was some writing on the box, but it was far too tiny for Kendra to read.

"This must be Skeezle," Kendra declared. "But how is he ever going to help you, Mr. Hagglehorn?"

"He's not," Effryn replied. "I never said he would, did I? But I just need him to get close enough so that I can touch him. Then I'll be able to get myself out of this quandary."

"Well, Trooogul and I can help speed up this affair," Kendra declared.

Ever so gently, the Een girl scooped the snail into her hands. Then, she handed the shelled creature to Trooogul who, being much taller than Kendra, was able to pass it up to Effryn.

"Ah, much obliged!" the Faun said, accepting Skeezle into his plump hands. Then he cried, "Ta-wit-cha-doo-roo!"

In that instant, there was a great puff of smoke—and when it cleared, Skeezle had grown from a very tiny snail into a simply enormous one, so big that he towered above even Trooogul. The box had grown too, though now, Kendra could see that it was not so much a box, but rather a type of carriage that was attached to the back of the snail. The words on the side of the carriage were now plainly visible. They read:

Effryn Hagglehorn's Marvelous Marvels
Cures, Charms, Curios ~ Cheap!

While Kendra and Trooogul were still gaping at this sudden spectacle of magic, Effryn reached into the carriage (he was now hanging right alongside it) and lifted out a sharp tool, which he then used to cut himself free. He landed to the ground with a soft plop. He picked himself up and, after brushing the dirt out of his beard, announced, "Well, let's open shop, shall we?"

CHAPTER 23

Effryn Hagglehorn's
Marvelous
Marvels

Hopefully,

you've never had the
misfortune in your life
of having to talk your
way out of a deal with
a huckster. What is
a "huckster," you ask?
Well, a huckster is
someone who can
sell anything to
anyone—and if
Kendra had ever met
a huckster, well, then, it
was Effryn Hagglehorn.

Before Kendra could
even ask the fat little Faun
what "shop" he was referring
to, Effryn had trotted over to
Skeezle and snapped his fingers,
which caused the sides of the carriage
to burst open and reveal a glistening
heap of caskets, flasks, cauldrons, urns, chests,
horns, and jugs, all bound haphazardly together

with twine. Indeed, it looked as if removing just one item would mean the collapse of the entire mound of curios—but this was exactly what Effryn did. Leaping upon the stack with his little hooves, he began yanking out a bottle here and a flask there and tossing them down to Kendra and Trooogul as he prattled on about his many wares.

"How about the dust from a fairy's freckle? A gnome's drone? The blink of a dragon's eye?"

Kendra and Trooogul stared at each other, shrugging helplessly.

"Perhaps an Izzard's cough?" Effryn called down. "Or an Orrid's bad breath? Both very good for treating Goojun pox—or so I hear."

Kendra ventured a look over at Skeezle, but the oversized snail showed not the slightest interest in any of his master's chatter. His long antennae bobbed as Effryn scrambled back and forth across the carriage strapped to his back. It didn't appear as if Skeezle could talk—but Kendra was sure that she saw the great slug yawn.

"What? Nothing shakes your soda yet?" Effryn asked, looking down at them from his pile. "Well, trim my tail! You two make a pair of poor consumers."

"Sorry, Mr. Hagglehorn," Kendra spoke up. "We don't exactly have any money."

"No money!" Effryn cried, hopping down from his carriage. "Well, run a razor over my rump! Why the heck did you come to see me then?"

"We didn't!" Kendra replied. "Don't you remember? We *found* you."

"Helpedzum little Faunee, as matter of factzum," Trooogul added gruffly.

"Helped me?" Effryn said, jabbing a finger at them. "Well, I didn't ask you, did I? And you certainly didn't negotiate anything in return for your assistance. So I do believe, in the absence of any formal contract, that you can't hold me to any sort of remuneration."

"Well—of course not—we didn't expect anything," Kendra sputtered. "But—,"

"Maybe Trooogul just squishee Faunee," Trooogul snorted, lifting one of his massive fists.

"There's no need to be uncivil," Effryn said, shirking beneath the shadow of the beast's giant claw. "But listen, I'll tell you what. I have something for you, Kendra. Something that an Een would want—very much, I suspect."

"And what is that?" Kendra asked curiously.

"Why, do you see this?" Effryn asked, producing a small silver bottle. "Inside is a magic little whisper I found bouncing back and forth in a quiet corner of Echo Valley last October. It was trapped there, you see! Couldn't get out. And I managed

to scoop it into this bottle—the secret of the magic curtain that protects the land of Een from the outside world!"

Kendra let out a shriek. "You have to give that to me!" she cried, reaching for the bottle, but just as quickly, Effryn slipped it into some mysterious pocket on his person.

"Well, wax my whiskers!" the Faun cried. "I do believe you want this after all."

"Of course I do!" Kendra said excitedly. "The secret of the magic curtain was inside the Box of Whispers, until it escaped with the rest of the secrets of Een. But it rightfully belongs to Een. You ought to give it back."

"I'll do no sort of thing," Effryn retorted. "But I will *sell* it."

"Can Trooogul squishee Faunee nowzum?" Trooogul asked Kendra, lifting his fist again.

"Now, now," Effryn said. "How'd you like me to turn you into a rock, eh Trooogul? I can do it, you know! Besides, I'm just trying to conduct a business transaction here."

"But you can't sell what's not yours!" Kendra said.

"But it *is* mine," Effryn said. "Finders keepers."

"You're . . . you're as greedy as a Dwarf!" Kendra told him.

"Now you injure my feelings," Effryn said, kicking at the ground with his hooves. "If I was greedy, I'd be selling the spell of the magic curtain to the highest bidder, wouldn't I? But I'm offering it to an Een, aren't I? I could quite as easily walk up to Izzard City or Krake Castle; those critters would pay a heap of gold for this little spell."

"No listenzum to Faunee," Trooogul said, stepping in between Kendra and Effryn. "Faunee knowzum that beasties likezum Izzards, Krakes, and Ungers no havezum gold."

"Well, not as much as Een," Effryn admitted with a twitch of his big goat ears.

"That may be true," Kendra said. "But this is one Een who doesn't have *any* gold."

"Then I tell you what," Effryn said, a twinkle growing in his eye. "What you need to do is take me to that land of Een of yours, Kendra. It's hidden from me of course, because I'm not an Een. But if you can get me there, well then I'm sure the Een Elders will pay handsomely for this secret! After all, they don't want it falling into the wrong hands . . . or, should I say, claws?"

"Is that some sort of threat?" Kendra asked.

"Of course not," Effryn bleated. "I'm just asking you to take me to Een, so I can sell my wares."

"But we're not going to Een," Kendra said. "We're headed for the Door to Unger."

"Well, I'll be shorn!" Effryn cried, leaping back and crashing right into Skeezle, so that a small chest from the top of the carriage fell down and bounced off his hairy head.

"Whyzum Faunee always talking about gettings shorn or shavezum?" Trooogul asked. "Itzum annoying."

"Well, no self-respecting Faun ever wants to be shaved," Effryn replied, rubbing the spot on his head where he had been struck. "Why, we're a hairy folk, us Fauns, and we like it that way. But I think I do need to go to the barber and get the hair clipped out of my ears. Because what I thought you said, Kendra, was that you *wanted* to go to the Door to Unger."

"You heard right," Kendra told the funny creature. "I do want to go to the door. My uncle and my friends have been taken there. And it's up to me to . . . to . . . well, save them, and destroy that wretched place."

"Butter my beard!" Effryn cried. "From what I've heard, anyone who's ever gone to the Door to Unger has never come back! What makes you think you're any different? And why would Trooogul want to destroy the door? Just what are you two up to anyway?"

Kendra wasn't sure she could trust the strange little Faun, but she decided the best thing to do would be tell him the whole story. And so, that's what she did. She told him of the Unger prophecy, how she was marked on her palm, and how the Unger Oroook had told her that she needed to get to the door before the first summer's moon.

"It's quite a tale," Effryn said, when she had finished. "Now, I've heard of this Unger prophecy, of course. Why, I'm sure I have a copy of it somewhere in my carriage—I'll sell it to you if you want."

"We don't need it, thanks," Kendra said, giving her braids a tug of frustration. "What we really need is to get to the door as soon as possible."

"That's true," Effryn mused. "Summer is but a few days away—which means the first moon of the season."

"Oroook said the door only opens once a year—on that night, in fact," Kendra said.

"Well, you can make it in time, if you hurry," Effryn remarked as he scratched his hairy chin.

"Do you know the way?" Kendra asked.

"Of course!" Effryn answered. "I know everything—for a price of course. But you'll need more than my sense of direction to succeed, that's for sure."

"How so?" Kendra asked.

"Well, the keepers of the door aren't just going to let you skip up and walk through it," Effryn said.

"Wezum no needzum Faunee's helpzum," Trooogul growled. "Trooogul been thinkingzum aboutzum plan."

186

"Well, knot my nose hair!" Effryn brayed. "An Unger with a plan. Let's hear it!"

"Trooogul pretend-zum Eenee is prisoner and takezum her to door-zum," the Unger said.

"That's a great idea, Trooogul," Kendra said.

"Is it, though?" Effryn asked. "And what are you going to do about the mark on your palm? If the Ungers see it—and they will—why, they'll never let you near the door."

Kendra cast a look of despair at Trooogul. "He's right," she said.

"Well, look—I can help you, after all," Effryn said, putting his stubby arm around Kendra's shoulder. "I can give you something that will disguise the mark. It's a magic ointment. A little dab of that on your palm and no beasties will be able to see that pesky sign."

"And how much will that cost?" Kendra wondered.

"Why, I've already told you," Effryn said. "When all of this business is done, you must lead me back to the land of Een. Consider it a trade."

"But I don't know if I can do that," Kendra said. "Outsiders aren't welcome in Een."

"Why, I'm a Faun," Effryn announced. "Fauns and Eens have a long history, don't we? My ancient ancestor, Flavius Faun, made his home in the land of Een, hundreds of years ago, before you closed off the place with that curtain of yours. You yourself said there's a statue of him, right in the middle of town."

"Yes," Kendra said, "but that doesn't mean—well, look, that's the least of our problems. Who knows what's going to happen once we reach the door? We might all be destroyed! Then you won't get anything, Mr. Hagglehorn. Are you really ready to take that chance?"

"Look at it this way," Effryn said. "If you don't come back—well, I suppose I haven't lost much except for a dab of ointment. But if you do come back, then it's off to Een . . . and I'll be rich, rich, rich! I'll finally be able to take my children on that holiday they're always nagging me about."

"Thoughtzum Faunee say no havezum kiddeez," Trooogul accused.

"Did I?" Effryn asked with a nervous flick of his tail. "Well, that's not the point, is it? The point is to strike a deal that makes everyone happy."

Kendra sat down on a nearby rock and toyed nervously with her brother's compass. She wished, somehow, that it could show her the way to the door, the way to the right decision. If only it could tell her whether or not to accept Effryn's offer. Here she was, in the middle of nowhere, and her only companions were an Unger and a Faun—neither of whom she was sure she could trust. Everything seemed so difficult, so improbable. She felt the odds were stacked against her.

CHAPTER 24

Madness at Midnight

Sometimes,

when you are faced with a grave decision, you just have to end up trusting your instincts. This is what Kendra did now. Somehow she had the feeling that she would not succeed in finding the Door to Unger unless she accepted Effryn's deal. At last, she agreed to his plan: the strange little Faun would help her sneak into the Greeven Wastes, and when her mission was accomplished, she would take him to the land of Een.

When this was settled, Kendra and her new companions set onwards through the wilderness, towards the Door to Unger. They made a motley crew, to be sure: a tiny Een girl, a furry little Faun, a giant snail, and a mighty Unger, all in procession.

At first Kendra thought Skeezle would slow them down, for after all, he was a snail. However, it appeared that the great slug was magical in more ways than one, for he plowed forward at such a pace that Kendra was forever panting to keep up. At last, Effryn invited her to ride atop the huge slug, and she gladly accepted his offer.

They traveled without adventure for the next two days. The temperature continued to drop and the wind became stronger and louder, howling across the landscape like some angry beast. Kendra pulled her ragged cloak tighter around her frail body and hoped it would all be over soon. That night, they set up camp against the flat side of a large jagged rock that pointed like an arrowhead towards the sky.

"Maybe this will shield us from the wind a bit," Effryn announced. "And any beasties out there too. Because we're close to that door now. I reckon we'll reach the edge of the Wastes by noon tomorrow."

As was his custom each night, Effryn shrunk Skeezle and hid him nearby; according to the Faun, this was the best way to safe keep his precious carriage of magic marvels, for it was hard for anyone to steal that which was too small to see. With this act accomplished for the evening, they all settled down to pass a cold and quiet night, huddled against the rock.

It was only a few hours later when Kendra awoke with a sudden start. She had heard a voice and her immediate suspicion was that someone had stolen upon their camp. She turned to rustle Trooogul, but the great Unger was already awake.

"You heard it too then?" she asked.

"Yeezum," Trooogul replied. "But wherezum Faunee?"

Kendra then realized that Effryn was nowhere to be seen. Had he abandoned them? Then she heard the voice again—it was coming from the very top of the rock. She and Trooogul stepped back to get a better view—and there was Effryn himself, perched like a little goat on top of the blunted point of the boulder and braying at the moon.

"Whatsee Faunee doingzum?" Trooogul asked.

"I don't know!" Kendra replied, yanking on her braids.

They called up to the peculiar creature, but he did not respond. Even from the bottom of the rock, Kendra could see that the Faun's eyes were wild and crazed, and strange words were spewing forth from his lips.

"Truth!" Effryn proclaimed. "The truth is inside of you! If you don't trust in the truth then you will become one of them, Kandlestar!"

"Mr. Hagglehorn!" Kendra cried. "Are you talking to me?"

The Faun looked down at her, his eyes wide and green with excitement. "Kandlestar!" he shouted, his ears twitching. "You must trust; you must believe."

"Believezum what?" Trooogul demanded irritably.

"You have to believe what you *know*, not what they *tell you*," Effryn proclaimed from the top of his rocky berth. "Don't you see?"

"I don't understand at all," Kendra declared.

"Faunee gonezum crazee," Trooogul grunted.

"Believe, I tell you, believe!" Effryn bleated. "It's the only way—or I'll be shorn! But mind this, Kandlestar. Many will go into the maze—but not all will make it out. One will be left behind."

"Who?" Kendra cried. "What are you talking about?"

But Effryn had no answer for her. Suddenly his eyes glazed over and he toppled over the side of the steep rock. Luckily, Trooogul was there to catch the Faun in his strong arms.

"Lay him on the ground!" Kendra cried frantically.

Trooogul did so and Kendra knelt over to wipe Effryn's forehead with a handkerchief. His entire face was drenched in perspiration and he was trembling head to hoof. Then, just like that, Effryn sat up and looked at Kendra and Trooogul with surprise.

"Well, braid my beard!" he exclaimed. "What are you two doing, staring at a fellow who's just trying to get some winks?"

"You haven't been sleeping," Kendra told the Faun. "You've been moaning at the moon!"

"Oh dear," Effryn murmured, taking Kendra's handkerchief and mopping his brow. "Did it happen again?"

"Did what happen?" Kendra asked.

"Sometimes I have these mad moonlight visions," Effryn explained. "They're like dreams, but they seem to take over my entire body."

"Nozum kidding," Trooogul snorted.

"How often do you have these, er . . . visions?" Kendra inquired of the Faun.

"A lot lately, I'm afraid," Effryn said. "I had one the night before you met me, to tell the truth. That's how I came to be caught in that snare. I went to sleep, same as always, and awoke the next morning in that trap. During the night I must have had one of my spells and ended up stepping into the snare."

"I think you need to see a healer," Kendra said.

"A healer?!" Effryn blurted, rising to his hooves. "Why, I'm the best healer around! But no, no—there's no cure for me."

"What do you mean?" Kendra asked.

"Why, it's an old Hagglehorn trait, these spells," Effryn explained. "My own grandpappy used to get them, sure as you're shorn. Folks used to say he was a prophet. They used to heed his words like they were gospel. There was wisdom in his gibberish—and there is in mine too. It's just that I can't ever remember what I say."

"I do," Kendra said. "You called my name. You said that I had to believe in what I know and . . . and . . . that many would go into the maze, but someone wasn't going to make it out."

"Well, you heed my words, whatever I said," Effryn told her. "It might help you before this adventure's out—that much I'm sure of. And you were given my vision for free! My grandpappy used to charge folks for making use of his prophecies."

"Surezum," Trooogul grumbled.

Kendra sighed and gave one of her braids an extra hard tug. "Do you really believe in all of this prophecy business, Mr. Hagglehorn?" she asked.

"Well," Effryn replied, "the Ungers sure do. And as my grandpappy used to say: 'Horns and hooves are as strong as stone, but the heart is stronger yet.'"

"What does that mean?" Kendra wondered.

"It means nothing in this world is as strong as belief," Effryn explained.

———

As Effryn had predicted, by noon of the next day the rag-tag band of travelers had reached the edge of the Greeven Wastes. There was no mistaking their arrival at this dreadful place, for it was as if all life—whether it be tree, bush, or even blade of grass—ceased to exist, giving abruptly away to a vast and empty expanse of rock and rubble. Kendra stared upon this cold and desolate wilderness and felt her heart grow glum. To the tiny Een girl, the forlorn wastes seemed to stretch on forever, and yet she knew that somewhere across its weary barrens she would find her final destination, the Door to Unger.

She pulled her cloak tight, hoping to fend off the claws of the bone-chilling wind. "It's a horrid place," she murmured through chattering teeth.

"They don't call it the Wastes for nothing," Effryn remarked, almost too cheerfully for Kendra's liking. "Well, you two kids better get on with it. Skeezle and I will be waiting here for you."

"Are you sure you won't come with us?" Kendra asked.

"Who? Me?" Effryn asked. "Not on your life! I've skirted this deplorable desert many a time, but have never ventured in! Tangle my tail or wax my whiskers—but you won't get me to stick a single hoof upon that ghastly plain of rock and ruin."

"No let Faunee scarezum Eeneez," Trooogul said to Kendra, though he himself didn't seem at all eager to set forward.

"Well, come on, Mr. Hagglehorn," Kendra said finally, with a brave pull on her braids. "Let's see if we can hide my mark with that ointment of yours."

"Ah, yes," Effryn said. He climbed to the top of his carriage and began rooting through his mountain of magical marvels. "Now where did I put it?" he muttered as he began tossing out various bottles and canisters. "Was it next to the Centaur scent? Or with the Elf ale?"

"Maybe no go anytime soonzum," Trooogul sighed.

But in the next moment, Effryn had hopped back to the ground with a small round vial.

"Hold your hand out, Kendra," the Faun instructed.

Kendra obliged and Effryn rubbed a sweet-smelling salve upon her palm.

"Can you see the mark now?" Effryn asked Trooogul.

"Nozum!" the Unger replied with some surprise. "Itzum completely gonezum."

"Ah, it's not gone at all!" Effryn declared happily. "Just cleverly hidden."

"How long will it last?" Kendra asked.

"A few days anyway," Effryn replied. "And trust me—you don't want to find yourself in the Greeven Wastes any longer than that!"

It was now time to enact the next part of their plan. Effryn supplied them with a musty old sack, which Kendra climbed into and Trooogul then slung over his bony back, so that it might appear as if she was his prisoner. Kendra couldn't help but to be reminded of how Trooogul had carried her in the same way to escape the mines of Umbor.

"Just like old times," Kendra murmured, though she couldn't help to think that this time, instead of fleeing danger, they were headed straight towards it.

CHAPTER 25

The Keepers at the Door

The journey across the desolate Greeven Wastes soon became one long dreary blur for Kendra. The air was bitter and cold, and the sack uncomfortable. Even though Trooogul warned against it, she stuck her head out from time to time to look about—but she found little to interest her in the monotonous sea of rock that seemed to stretch in every direction. All she could do was pull her cloak tightly about her and try to block out the frigid air.

"I thought it was supposed to be summer soon," she grumbled.

"No thinkzum summer comezum here," Trooogul grunted in reply.

The journey continued. After what seemed like many hours, the landscape finally began to change. Now the two companions could see larger rocks scattered here and there amidst the flat sea of rubble. These were tall and straight, jutting up from the ground like great stone teeth. As Trooogul trudged onward, these rocks began to increase in number until there were soon so many of them that it was as if they were traveling through a dense forest. But this was a forest unlike Kendra had ever seen, for there were no trees or plants here; this was a forest made completely of stone columns, tall and cold and gray.

"This place gives me the creeps," Kendra murmured.

"Must shutzum now," Trooogul warned her. "Wezum getzum close. Must pretendzum that Eeneez and Trooogul arezum enemies."

"I thought we were enemies," Kendra said light-heartedly.

"Little Eenee knows whatzum Trooogul mean," the Unger said solemnly.

"I know," Kendra returned. "I was just joking."

But he said nothing more and it seemed to Kendra as if he had suddenly become very sad. Part of her understood why, for she felt the same way. For the past few weeks she and Trooogul had entered into a strange fellowship, working together to find their way to the door. They had encountered many adventures and overcome a few formidable challenges. And, despite her suspicions of the great beast, Kendra could not help but to feel friendship towards Trooogul. Now that they were on the brink of reaching the Door to Unger, Kendra knew everything would change. No matter what happened now, their friendship would never be the same.

As these thoughts meandered through her mind, Kendra watched the dreary wall of stone columns go by. Then, to her great surprise, she noticed one of the massive pillars move. She gave her head a shake. Had she seen right? She looked again and suddenly realized that many of the tall standing stones were not stones at all—but Ungers! There gray chiseled bodies made them look just like mighty rocks, and they blended right in with the forest of columns.

"Trooogul!" Kendra whispered.

But Trooogul had already seen them. He came to a stop, and now the Ungers suddenly came to life, stepping forth from the forest of stone to block their way. Kendra could see that they were armed with clubs, and axes, and spears, and some of them even wore pieces of battered gray armor. Instinctively, she wriggled down in the sack, as if somehow she would be safe from the beasts if only they could not see her.

Then Kendra heard one of the Unger guards speak. "Youzum, Unger," the guard snarled at Trooogul. "Whyzum comes to Wastes of Greeve?"

"Trooogul bringzum Eeneez for Door to Unger," Trooogul replied, and Kendra felt him lift the sack and shake it before them. She let out a little shriek and the guards grunted in satisfaction.

"Trooogul just in timezum," the guard said. "Ceremonee is tomorrowzum. Youzum come now. Wezum takes you tozum Keepers."

Keepers? Kendra wondered. *Who are they?*

She felt Trooogul swing the sack back over his shoulder. She hated not being able to see, and after a moment, she mustered the courage to poke her head out of the sack. She watched as they trudged through the stone forest, this time escorted by a parade of Ungers. Before long, their way turned up into a great jumble of rocks. As they snaked through this great pile of stone, the light began to grow dim, and Kendra realized that night was falling. She gave her braids a fretful tug and did her best to stay calm, despite her fear. She could now see many other creatures skittering about the rocks; these were mostly Ungers, but there were also other beasts: Orrids and Krakes and Goojuns and Izzards.

It's just one big monster bash, Kendra grimaced to herself.

Before long one of the guards announced, "Wezum arrive. Trooogul now takezum Eenee tozum Keepers."

Kendra heard Trooogul grunt something in reply, and the Unger scuttled forward, down a long flight of steps to a vast chamber. Trooogul reached the bottom of the stairs, gave the sack a shake, and emptied Kendra so roughly that she tumbled head over heels onto the hard, stony ground. Slowly, she pulled herself to her feet and gathered her wits in an effort to get a better look at her surroundings. She could now see that they had arrived at a place not unlike a large open-air stadium that had been built within the rocks. Behind her, stretching up towards the vast night sky, were the seats (which were currently unoccupied) and in front of her was a ledge of rock—a stage, if you will. Here sat a row of Unger Elders—at

least, they looked like Elders to Kendra. Their faces were thin and gaunt, and their hair was ghostly white. Each held a long wooden staff decorated with beads and feathers. These Elders sat in a semicircle before her, six of them in all, though there was a seventh seat conspicuously empty.

Who's missing? Kendra wondered.

But the only other Unger in the room was Trooogul. He was standing behind her, and Kendra now realized that she was being presented to this grotesque assembly of Elders as if she was some sort of trophy.

Much to Kendra's surprise, the Elders said nothing. They did not even seem to notice her; rather, they stared blankly ahead into the night. When Kendra looked past them, she now noticed a great wall of rock rising up behind them. It was carved with the shape of a mighty face—but it was not any face.

"Why, it's an Een!" Kendra gasped.

In fact, the carving looked like many of the faces she had seen sculpted into the walls of the Elder Stone, back in her beloved land of Een. This face, here in the Greeven Wastes, towered above the little girl and she could not help but notice that its most prominent feature was its mouth, for it was tall and wide and fitted with long slats of weathered wood that seemed like rough gray teeth, crossed with thick iron braces. It looked like a door—though a strange one indeed, for there was no handle, no knocker, and no apparent way to open it. Then Kendra realized what she was looking at.

"The Door to Unger!" she murmured as quietly as she could, despite her excitement. "We've found it."

Then, with a sudden rocky ripple, the great stone face came alive and began to speak, its stone whiskers and lips moving around its great wooden teeth.

"Welcome to the Door to Unger," the face intoned. "Come before me, Ungerling, and show me your quarry."

Trooogul gave Kendra a nudge with one of his mighty claws and she stumbled forward, towards the door. Still the Unger Elders did not move, and Kendra saw Trooogul cast them a nervous glance.

"Show no fear of them," the door said.

It spoke in a slow, ponderous voice, but one that was laced with a temper, as if it was doing its very best to try and contain a furious rage that bubbled beneath the surface. To Kendra, the door seemed like it might erupt in fury at any moment.

Then Trooogul asked boldly, "Whozum Elders?"

"These are the Keepers of the Door to Unger," the door responded. "They have pledged their lives to protect me from all who would seek to destroy me. They wait in silence for the night of Greeve, when once a year all prisoners are cast through my maw and into my belly."

Kendra gave her braids a desperate tug of fear. She looked up at Trooogul, but the young Unger was still gazing upon the Unger Elders.

"Theirs is a vow of silence," the door said. "They do my bidding alone. To sit on the council of Keepers is a great honor. Maybe you, young Unger, will one day receive such an honor. The fact that you have brought a prize before me makes you worthy."

Then the door seemed to turn its attention to Kendra. "Ah . . . a young one," it said, and then, in a more threatening voice: "Raise your hands, beast!"

With a start, Kendra leapt backwards, only to feel Trooogul's rough claw against her spine. She lifted her hands, palms open, to the door.

"Goooood," the door droned. "You are clean, pitiful Een. You are worthy for Unger!"

"NOZUM!" came a voice.

Kendra whirled around to see an Unger burst into the stadium, as if in a great panic. He charged down the stairs towards the stage, but now, at last, the Keepers showed signs of life. With surprising quickness, they pounced to their feet and soon had the Unger intruder surrounded, their staffs at the ready.

"What is the meaning of this?!" the door boomed. "Who dares to interrupt the presentation of a prisoner?"

Kendra stared hard at the Unger. Somehow, he seemed familiar. She cast a glance at Trooogul, only to see that all the color had drained from his face. He, too, had recognized this Unger intruder. Then it came to Kendra: The intruder was Creeegun.

What is he doing here? Kendra wondered, but before she had even finished asking herself the question, she knew the answer. *Of course,* she thought. *He brought Uncle Griffinskitch and the others to the door. And now he's seen me—and he knows I'm the forbidden one. Everything is ruined.*

Creeegun pointed a crooked claw at Kendra, murderous hatred in his eyes. "Creeegun comezum to protect doorzum," he announced, his nostrils flaring with rage. "Protectzum door fromzum traitor!"

The door seemed to consider this news, his face twisting in the rock with a pensive fury. At long last it said, "Speak then, Ungerling. For I do not take kindly to those who would betray me."

Kendra gulped. In an eerie moment of realization, she suddenly knew why one chair in the council of Keepers was empty. It had belonged to the Unger Oroook, the very beast who had set off this entire chain of events by coming to visit her on that stormy night that now seemed so long ago. That chair had not been long vacated, Kendra knew. The other Keepers had killed Oroook and had yet to replace him on their council.

The Keepers now lowered their staffs and allowed Creeegun to approach the door.

"Eenee thatzum stand herezum is forbidden onezum," Creeegun accused. "Eeneez marked with starzum!"

"Unger talkzum nonsense," Trooogul spoke up angrily. "Keepers seezum hand! Therezum no mark."

"A trick?" the door wondered. "Keepers—look upon her hands again!"

The Unger Keepers moved forward and struck Kendra with their staffs, forcing her to show her hands once again. Kendra gulped again and closed her eyes tightly. She prayed that Effryn's ointment would stand their scrutiny. But the Keepers studied her palms for only a moment. Then all six turned to the Door and shook their heads.

"No mark!" the door bellowed. "Tell me, young Creeegun, what possesses you to spread such a tale?"

Creeegun, however, seemed too confused to answer. He stared at Kendra, his gray brow knotted in bewilderment.

"Creeegun no wantzum sharezum honor," Trooogul said to the door. "Thatzum why Creeegun tellzum wild liezum."

"Ah! A seeker of glory, is it?" the Door asked. "Shame on you, Creeegun! Many Eens have you brought to me on the eve of our dark festival. Relished in this honor long you should have and not begrudged your fellow Unger his one measly Een child that he would present before me."

"Butzum—"

"There is no 'but'!" the door cried. "Keepers! Take this sorry Unger from my sight! He shall not witness the festival of Greeve!"

"No! Pleazum!" Creeegun moaned, but at once the Keepers began beating him with their staffs. Creeegun cast one final perplexed glance at Kendra. Then, he lowered his head in shame and scampered out of the stadium.

Kendra let out a sigh of relief. *So far, so good,* she thought.

"Now," the door said, the satisfaction clear in its tone, "back to our business at hand. Trooogul, go make yourself merry. Feast and prepare for the festival of Greeve. Keepers, take this disgusting Een and cast her into the dungeon. Tomorrow, she shall know Unger!"

At this command, one of the Keepers reached out and, grabbing Kendra by her long braids, lifted her from the ground and carried her away. She kicked her legs and cried in pain (for it hurt to be carried so), but the Keeper showed no reaction. He lumbered through a series of dark and winding passageways until he came to a small door set within the rocks. With a flick of his claw he struck some lever in the wall and the door sprang open. Brusquely, he tossed her inside and the door slammed shut behind her.

Inside the chamber was black as a hole, but even though Kendra couldn't see a thing, she immediately knew she was not alone. She could hear rustling in the dark. Someone—or *something*—was alive in there.

CHAPTER 26

An Unhappy Reunion

Kendra

reached out into the darkness, groping to find her way around the dungeon cell. "Hello?" she asked meekly.

"Eek!" a voice replied. "Who is it?"

"Oki!" Kendra cried. "Is that you?"

She rushed blindly into the darkness and soon found the small gray mouse in her arms. She embraced him tightly, crying with joy. Then she heard other voices and the patter of feet; in the next minute, she found herself happily swarmed by her old friends.

As her eyes grew accustomed to the darkness their shapes took form and now she could see just how badly

207

they had suffered from their long journey to the Greeven Wastes. Oki and Ratchet looked scraggly and battered, while one of Jinx's antennae was bent nearly in half, and Professor Bumblebean's spectacles sported a crooked crack. But none looked worse than old Uncle Griffinskitch. His skin was pale, his eyes were dull, and his beard seemed a tangled mess of white hair.

The only thing he had not lost, it seemed, was his grumpiness, for upon seeing Kendra he said, "Just what in the name of Een are you doing here, child?"

"Why, I came to rescue you, of course," Kendra said.

Uncle Griffinskitch raised an eyebrow at her. "Humph," he muttered. "Marvelous work."

"Well, I'm glad to see you, at least," Kendra retorted.

"I wish I could say the same!" the old man reproached her, waving a stern finger in her direction.

"And what's that supposed to mean?" Kendra demanded.

"It means the only thing that has kept me going all this while was the knowledge that you weren't with us!" Uncle Griffinskitch growled. "I thought you were safe."

"I am safe," Kendra declared.

"Uh, Kendra," Oki said. "You realize we're in a dungeon, right? In the middle of the Greeven Wastes?"

"He's right," Ratchet added. "You didn't bump your head or something, did you?"

"Of course not!" Kendra said. "Don't you understand? This is all just a trick! The Ungers don't want me here. I snuck in!"

"My word!" Professor Bumblebean exclaimed, pushing his glasses up the slope of his nose. "Do you mean to say you *willingly* conducted this expedition to the Greeven Wastes?"

Kendra nodded. "Trooogul helped me."

"Days of Een!" Uncle Griffinskitch boomed. "That Unger, you mean?"

"Yes," Kendra said, and she went on to tell them the whole story, explaining how she had escaped the Mines of Umbor with Trooogul's help, how she had found Kiro's compass, and how Effryn had helped them sneak into the Greeven Wastes.

The news about Kendra's brother seemed too much for Uncle Griffinskitch to bear. Kendra passed him the tarnished compass and the old Een sat down on a small stone to gaze sadly upon it. "He wanted to be an explorer, that boy," Uncle Griffinskitch murmured softly. "It's all he ever talked about. This compass was meant to keep him from getting lost. Aye, but it did not work. He's been lost to me for nearly twelve years."

"Now we can find him!" Kendra urged, grabbing her uncle's arm. "Don't you see? Kiro was brought to the Greeven Wastes. This compass proves it! He lost it on the way."

"What does it matter now?" the old wizard asked sadly.

"The door is the key to this whole mystery," Kendra declared. "Kiro went through that door and now I'm going to go through it, too. Except I'm going to destroy it—just like the prophecy said. I'll find out what happened to our family, Uncle Griffinskitch. I'll get us all out of here."

"If you really wanted to get us out of here, you just should have brought a sword or two," Jinx declared. "Then I could have slashed our way out of this miserable dump."

"Humph," Uncle Griffinskitch muttered, but it was a humph filled more with sorrow than with anger. "Listen," he said, looking at Kendra. "I don't trust this Unger prophecy. In fact, I don't trust Ungers."

"You trusted Oroook enough for us to go on this journey," Kendra pointed out.

"Indeed!" the old wizard grumbled. "And now look what has become of us. It was my hope that we could find the door and *choose* what to do next. But now we have no choice. We shall be tossed through it whether we want to or not."

"Trooogul and I've got everything under control," Kendra said. "You'll see."

"I don't want to see!" Uncle Griffinskitch declared hotly. "How many people must I lose to these dreadful Ungers! They've taken my whole family, everyone except you, Kendra. And yet, here you are; now they've taken you, too."

"It's not like that," Kendra persisted. "You're not listening. Trooogul didn't take me . . . he's helping me."

"But Kendra!" Professor Bumblebean exclaimed. "How can you trust this . . . this . . . this . . . monster?!"

"Are you sure he just didn't trick you to come here?" Oki asked Kendra. "Maybe it was just his way of getting you to go through the door."

210

Uncle Griffinskitch shook his weary head and clutched Kiro's compass to his breast. "I'm afraid this door will be the doom of us all," he murmured.

Kendra stared glumly at her friends. She knew they didn't trust Trooogul—or any Unger. How could they? After being carried across the Greeven Wastes by Creeegun and his cohorts, it was only natural that their hatred and fear of Ungers had grown. But they didn't know Trooogul, not like she did.

He didn't betray me, Kendra told herself, toying worriedly with her braids. But as she settled down for a cold and dismal night, a tiny niggling doubt whispered in her mind. She remembered how strangely Trooogul had acted in the underwater cave; he had known that the cave existed and yet at the same time claimed to know nothing of her brother. She thought about how sad he had seemed carrying her across the Greeven Wastes. It was almost as if he had been grappling with some great dilemma. Did he know she was going to her doom and was feeling bad about it, somehow?

Kendra let out a long sigh. There was only one thing she knew for sure, and that was this: tomorrow was the first moon of summer, and one way or the other, the truth would then be revealed.

By the time the Unger guards came the next day to retrieve Kendra and her companions, the sun was already sinking into the western horizon. They were made to march in line through the catacombs of the dungeons and up to the stadium. Uncle Griffinskitch was at the head of this sad procession, followed in order by Professor Bumblebean, Jinx, Ratchet, Oki, and, last of all, Kendra. During this short journey, they could hear the

hustle and bustle of the place, for it seemed as if every creature from the four corners of the known world had gathered in the stadium to witness the spectacle of their entry through the door.

As they were ushered down the steps of the arena and onto the stage before the door, Kendra cast her eyes upon the great throng of monsters in the stands. It was like looking upon a plague of claws and fangs and horns, for the beasts were crawling and skittering over top each other in a great thrill of anticipation. Their eyes gleamed in the fading light, and the theatre vibrated with their snorts and growls and exuberant jeers. Most of them were Ungers, but Kendra could also see other beasts too: Goojuns, Izzards, and the rest. She scanned the horde for any sign of Trooogul, but there were so many creatures it was impossible to pick him out. But Kendra knew he was up there. She knew he was watching.

Looking upon this great swarm of monsters, Kendra could not help being reminded of the mines of Umbor, when she had set free such creatures from Pugglemud's gloomy dungeons. But such an act had not garnered any blessings from this swarm. They cared not that she had saved them from slavery; on the contrary, they now seemed to salivate at the thought of watching her march to her own dismal fate. Ah, it is a hard lesson for any of us; to realize that a deed performed will not necessarily be reciprocated in the way we might wish.

Kendra turned her attention to the Door to Unger. It glared down at its prisoners with glee, but for the time being, it said nothing. Standing before the door were the six Keepers, but of course, they too were silent.

"W-what's going to happen now?" squeaked Oki, looking over his shoulder at Kendra.

"I don't know," Kendra admitted. "But stay close, little one. I'll look after you."

"We'll look after each other," Oki added with a brave but quivering voice.

They waited there, standing uncomfortably before the mob of monsters. Then they heard a scream—a different type of scream, one not belonging to any of the dreadful creatures in the audience. Kendra turned her head and saw an Unger guard lumbering onto the stage; in one of his giant claws, he was holding a pitiful creature by the tail. It was this creature that had emitted the scream.

"That's a strange looking fellow," Ratchet declared.

"Why, it's Effryn!" Kendra exclaimed. It wasn't the first time she had seen the kicking little goat-like creature hanging upside down.

"Findzum little Faunee on outskirtsee of wastezum," the guard announced, throwing Effryn down before the door.

"Gooood," the door intoned. "And what shall we do with the wretched thing?"

At this question the monstrous crowd erupted with suggestions.

"Killzum!"

"Squishee!"

"Throwzee inzum door!"

At this last proposition a malicious smile stretched widely across the wooden teeth of the door. "Excellent," he uttered. "The Faun will know Unger!"

"Wait!" Effryn howled, and Kendra could see that the strange creature was desperately frightened. He was pouring with sweat and trembling from hoof to horn. "I have a deal for you!"

"A deal?" the door bellowed. "What deal could a sniveling ball of wool have for the great and mighty Door to Unger?!"

"It's Eens you want, isn't it?" Effryn asked. "Why, I can give them to you. A whole lot of them! You can knot my knuckle hair otherwise!"

"Effryn, NO!" Kendra screamed, suddenly realizing what the Faun was trying to do.

"I have the secret to the magic curtain!" Effryn told the door feverishly. "I'll give it to you, or I'll be shorn."

"Days of Een!" Uncle Griffinskitch cried.

"SILENCE!" the door roared, and the whole stadium seemed to come to a quiet halt. For the next few moments, the door seemed to consider Effryn's offer with interest, his great rocky brow wrinkling above his eyes. "Show it to me," he said at last. "Show me the secret."

"Well, I don't have it *with* me," Effryn said. "But—"

"LIAR!" the door screamed, so loudly that the Faun was bowled over. "I have no time for despicable little tricksters. You will know Unger, and that will be the end of it."

With this decree, the Keepers lifted Effryn from the ground and thrust him into line, right behind Kendra.

"How could you?!" Kendra demanded of the Faun. "You would betray all of Een?"

"I'm sorry," Effryn whimpered. "I-I-I don't know what to say."

"You're a poor friend," Kendra scolded him. "Where's Skeezle?"

"Out there, beyond the Wastes," Effryn moaned. "I had shrunk him for the night and hid him behind a rock. But then I had one of my mad spells—and that's how I was captured."

"It almost serves you right," Kendra retorted, but the Faun was trembling so badly now that he seemed to hardly hear her. "What is it now?" she asked.

"L-l-look!" Effryn bleated, pointing to the sky.

Kendra looked upwards and let out a gasp.

The first moon of summer had risen.

CHAPTER 27

Into a Maze of Monsters

The door chuckled, his voice deep and sinister. And now, as the light of the summer's first moon struck him, the face in the stone began to transform before their very eyes. The rocks shifted and groaned and the great face tripled in size—until at last it looked like an Een no longer, but like an Unger. It even had two stony tusks jutting out from either side of his mouth like a pair of mighty columns.

"I am the Door to Unger," the rocky face boomed. "I open but one night of the year, to celebrate the curse of Greeve. Come to me and know the truth. Enter me, and you will know UNGER!"

With these words, the great wooden teeth of the door lifted upwards to reveal a dark and inky black abyss. Kendra gulped and now she noticed that Uncle Griffinskitch and the rest of her companions were stepping towards the gaping mouth of the door. It was as if they were in some sort of trance. She tried to call out to them, but no sound seemed to come from her throat. Then she realized that she, too, was walking towards the door! It was as if she was moving by some strange impulse; she tried to stop her legs, but she could not. She watched her companions disappear through the door in front of her, one by one, and soon she was the last one left. From behind her, she could hear the monstrous spectators erupt into a frenzy of cheering and raucous laughter; the whole stadium seemed to be shaking with their noise. Then, the next thing she knew, she was stepping in between the door's two large tusks and—just like that—she was engulfed in darkness.

Everything was abruptly quiet. She turned to look behind her, but saw nothing other than a row of sturdy wooden slats. The door had closed behind her, and the arena, with its roaring throng of monsters, was gone. She had crossed through the door. She had entered the maze.

For a moment she sat there in the darkness, alone, clutching at her braids. There was no sign of Uncle Griffinskitch, Oki, or any of the others. *Where have they gone?* She wondered. *Could they disappear, just like that?*

The silence was eerie. She could hear a soft thumping, off in the distance. It was the only noise in the whole place, and somehow, it made the maze seem even quieter. Kendra pulled harder on her braids. The silence made her feel incredibly alone.

"What now?" she whispered, just to hear the sound of her own voice. She had half-expected the door to crumble the

moment she crossed its threshold; after all, didn't the prophecy say that she would destroy the door? But the door hadn't been destroyed; in fact, *nothing* had happened. Kendra stood there, helplessly, wondering what to do next. "Maybe I just have to find my way out of here," she told herself after a moment. She said this in the most cheerful voice she could rally, but she couldn't help to wonder if coming to the door was the biggest mistake she had ever made.

She tried to push this doubt to the back of her mind as she took a step forward. The maze was incredibly dark; she could barely see a thing. Still, she had a sense that the maze was enormous, the type of place where you could yell and your voice would echo on through the ages. She looked about for some clue that would tell her the right direction to take. Yet, it was so dark that when standing next to one wall, she couldn't see another. Kendra was used to feeling small in a big world, but now she felt tinier than ever.

At last, she chose a passageway and set off into the darkness, pressing her hand against the wall to orientate herself. She knew the trick in any maze was to not get lost, so she did her best to remember her route. Then, as she walked, she became aware of a voice. It seemed to come from nowhere and everywhere at once, and Kendra knew immediately that the voice belonged to the door.

"Are you lost, child?" the door asked.

She tried to ignore this question, but the door repeated it until at last she said stubbornly, "No, I am not!"

"You will be," the door uttered, a hint of satisfaction in its voice. "Fear this place, child. *They* will get you."

"Who?" she asked, regretting the question the moment it left her lips. She didn't want to play the door's game. She tried putting her hands to her ears, to block out the voice, but it had no effect. It was as if the voice was inside her head.

Then Kendra turned a corner and found herself face to face with an enormous Orrid. It was a disgusting creature, hunched and crooked and green, with narrow eyes framed by a pair of curled horns. She had caught the thing in the act of gnawing on a shard of yellow bone, and now it glared upon her with voracious hunger.

"Eenee!" it screeched. Then, it pounced towards her, like a flea or some insect.

Kendra shrieked and turned to run back the way she had come. Now she put no thought into her direction, taking every turn or gateway she could find in the wretched maze. Through all this, the door was laughing, and Kendra scowled in anger. The door was right; she was now completely lost. There was no way she could ever remember the parts of the maze where she had already been.

With the Orrid still in hot pursuit, Kendra saw a window set in the wall, just low enough to the floor for her to reach. She leapt up and grabbed the ledge with her small hands. She pulled herself through, only to land with a thud in another corner of the maze, this time face-to-face with a large Unger, covered head to foot in long white hair. It stared at her a moment with its cold blue eyes before letting out a ferocious roar. Kendra didn't pause. Quickly, she darted through his legs and down another stretch of passageway.

Her heart was beating like a drum. She could hear the Orrid skitter through the window—now she had both of the monsters after her. And still the door was laughing.

She rounded a corner and ran smack into a pile of rubble, part of a wall that had tumbled down long ago so as to block

the corridor. She fell to the ground from the force of the colli-sion, but just as quickly got up and began scrambling through the debris. She had noticed a few holes between the fallen stones that were just big enough for her to squeeze through. Just as she pulled her tiny legs through one of these spaces, Kendra heard the Orrid and Unger come upon the rubble, screeching with fury that they had missed their chance to catch her.

On the other side of the pile of rocks, Kendra let out a sigh of relief and wiped her arm against her smarting fore-head. It seemed she had escaped the beasts—at least, for the time being.

But the voice was another matter.

"See," the door said. "They will destroy you, these fiendish aberrations. They will not rest until all of Een is vanquished, each of its citizens destroyed."

"That's not true!" Kendra retorted (though it was strange to be speaking to no one but thin air). "We could live together, Eens and Ungers and such. We could be friends."

The door now laughed so hard that the halls and passage-ways of the maze shook, as if trembling by earthquake. Kendra pitched herself against the wall just to keep from falling down.

"Oroook once thought as much," the door said after a moment. "Foolish Unger! He believed in the *one*. But I had the Keepers destroy him for his treacherous ways. Such is the fate of all those who defy the truth."

Truth? Kendra thought. She remembered Effryn's warning from the night he had brayed at the moon. *You have to believe what you know, not what they tell you,* he had said. Suddenly, she felt her boldness swell. "It's not my truth," she declared brazenly. "I *know* that Ungers and Eens can get along."

"Really?" the door mocked. "Perhaps you should explain that to the Unger that just tried to crush you in its claws. Understand this, child: all things that crawl, fly, or swim this wretched earth are filled with hatred. That's what I know, all too well."

Kendra shook her head and set off down the passage, leaving behind the pile of rubble that had allowed her to escape from the Orrid and Unger. She knew she had to keep moving. She had to try and find a way out of the maze—and yet, she had this terrifying feeling that she was just winding her way deeper and deeper into the core of the dark labyrinth. It was so hard to concentrate, for all the while the voice was speaking. It was like a tap that wouldn't stop dripping. Kendra thought she would go crazy. She wanted to scream. Every turn of the maze seemed to be the same as the last. Soon she began to wonder if she was just going down the same passage, over and over again. How could she find the way out? And what had happened to Uncle Griffinskitch and her friends?

These thoughts had just crossed her mind when Kendra stepped into an intersection of passageways—and there she saw little Oki. He was trembling head to foot and his eyes were wild with fear.

"Oki!" Kendra cried.

"EEK!" the tiny mouse screamed, and he turned and darted down one of the black passages.

The door chuckled.

"Wait!" Kendra called, running after her friend.

But Oki did not wait. It was as if he didn't recognize Kendra, or as if he thought she was going to harm him. *This place has made him go mad,* Kendra thought. She chased Oki through the zigzagging course of the maze, but his legs were spinning like two propellers in a storm and she could gain no ground on him.

And then the little mouse disappeared around a bend, and before she could get there herself, Kendra heard Oki release a terrible squeal—replaced a moment later by a loud, satisfied grunt.

"Oki!" Kendra cried, skidding to a halt.

She tried to muster the courage to look around the corner—but before it came to this, a hideous sharp-nosed snout peered around the wall. An Izzard! Its eyes gleamed through the darkness and yellow drool dripped down from its fanged mouth. Kendra knew Oki was no more.

CHAPTER 28

KWho**endra**
LFound in the**abyrinth**

Have you ever been so angry that your rage seemed to overtake your entire body? Your face flushes red, your hands turn to fists, and your whole body quakes, like some volcano urging to explode. Well, this was exactly what happened to Kendra when she saw the Izzard, for she could only guess that it had eaten her tiny friend. The door was cackling hysterically, but Kendra could barely hear it, so intense was her fury. She let out the loudest, blood-curdling scream that her tiny body was capable of and, without even thinking, she began picking stones from the floor and hurling them at the Izzard. Kendra could think of nothing but attacking the beast. The Izzard tried to snap at her, but Kendra's assault was now coming so fast and furious that the creature had to skitter backwards, away from the barrage of stones. At last it turned and fled into the impenetrable blackness of the maze.

Coward! Kendra thought. She pursued the creature, but it had soon escaped her. She threw herself to the ground, exhausted and in tears.

The entire temple maze had rumbled with the door's laughter through all of this, but at last it paused and said, "Ah ha! And now *you* know what it is to feel hatred enter your heart. Now you would have revenge!"

"SHUT UP!" Kendra shouted.

She pulled herself to her feet and dashed through the maze again, as if she could somehow escape the voice. But it was as if it was pursuing her, consuming her with its dark words. Around every corner, every bend, through every doorway— the sinister voice was there. It was *everywhere*.

"You cannot escape what's inside of you!" the door gloated. "You hate them, these monsters! And they hate you."

"No!" Kendra sobbed. "Not all of them. Not Trooogul. He helped me."

"Trooogul?" the door asked. "Who? The Unger who delivered you here? And how do you think he helped you, foolish child? He has brought you here, to me!"

Kendra's mind swirled. "No," she murmured meekly. "You don't understand . . . "

"You're the one who doesn't understand," the door snapped. "Open up your mind and let me see into your heart. I will show you the truth."

And now, Kendra could feel the voice invading her very mind and entering her memories. She shook her head, trying to keep him out—but it was no use. The voice—the door—could see and know everything inside of her.

"Wait," the door said, suddenly pausing in its probe. "What is this? There's something strange here, in your memories . . . "

Kendra squeezed her eyes tight, as if this would somehow help to block him out. There were things she didn't want him to see, such as—

"Oroook!" the door gasped, and Kendra knew he had discovered her memory of that dark night when the Unger had come to visit her and Uncle Griffinskitch. "I see," the door purred softly after a moment. "He did find you, after all, that traitor Oroook. I thought the Keepers had been able to destroy him first. Creeegun was right. You, child, *are* the forbidden one. You tried to trick me."

"We *did* trick you," Kendra retorted. "I'm here, aren't I?"

"And what will you do, now that you're here?" the door sneered. "Why, go ahead, child! Destroy me!"

Kendra glared up into the darkness of the maze, her blood boiling. She didn't know what to do—and the door knew it. He had called her bluff.

"I thought as much," the door growled. "What can you do? Nothing! You will know Unger, child, like every other wretched Een who comes to me. I know what you tried to do. You thought you could befriend Trooogul and turn him against me, to betray me. But no Unger can befriend an Een. It's against their nature. They hate Eens! Don't you see? It is *you* that has been betrayed."

"Just because you say it, doesn't make it true," Kendra retorted. "You're wrong about Trooogul!"

"Am I now?" the door droned wickedly. "He's out there, a hero among his monstrous brethren, and you're in here . . .

with me. Oh, I'm afraid he did betray you. And I can prove it to you."

Deeper into her mind the door pried, feasting on the memories of her Unger friend. He could see her saving Trooogul from the mines of Umbor, he could see them journey together, he could see them hiding in the cave . . .

"Ah," the door murmured with deep satisfaction. "The cave! Remember the cave, child? How do you think Trooogul came to be there before? You know how. He said he didn't remember. A lie, I expect. Oh, he was there before. Indeed, he probably helped capture your brother. He probably helped destroy your family!" He laughed, again so loud that the whole maze trembled. "How dim-witted and naive can you be?" he roared with glee. "You helped the very beast who destroyed your family! How stupid of you! How stupid of you!"

He repeated this last statement, over and over again, and now, the voice became Kendra's own.

"How stupid! How stupid!" she mumbled hysterically. She could feel her heart balloon with hatred. She felt as if she would explode in a fit of rage.

"I will delve deeper into your mind," the door said, "for there lay the darkest truths, the ones locked away in the quiet corners of your memory. We'll find things you can't even consciously remember, things you don't want to remember. But I can make you see them. I can help you remember the frightening truths of the past . . . "

In frustration, Kendra clenched fistfuls of hair in her hands, trying to resist. It was no use; she felt the voice probe her mind again and now the pictures came alive in her head. It was as if she was watching a performance or a play—except she was one of the actors, and she was watching from within

the scene. And in this scene Kendra was staring up into the face of a young Een boy, only five or six years old. He wasn't returning her gaze though; it was as if he was cradling her against his chest and it felt as though he was running, or rather scrambling, as if over a rugged landscape. *How can such a small boy carry me?* she wondered. *And why do I feel so . . . so . . . so tiny?* But then she realized that she wasn't an eleven-year-old girl in the vision. This was a memory from long, long ago. She was just a baby, and the boy was her brother, Kiro, and that's why he could carry her. She now realized she was wrapped in a green blanket; she couldn't move her hands or legs. She looked past Kiro's face, but all she could see was the sky, which seemed wild and forlorn. Then she became aware of a sound—the sound of Ungers. Now Kendra understood clearly: this was the memory of how her family had been taken by Ungers, and how she had been left behind. She watched in awe as the remainder of the scene unfolded in her mind's eye.

Kiro now came to a stop, his back against a large boulder. The sounds of the pursuing Ungers were growing louder; at any moment they would have them in their clutches. Kendra, as a helpless baby in the memory, looked upon her brother's face again. His cheeks were flushed red, his eyes wild with terror.

"We're trapped," he murmured feverishly, clutching Kendra tightly. "They're all around us. They've already got our folks! Why don't they just let us go?"

In the memory, Kendra longed to talk, to say something to him; but she could not, of course, for she was just a baby.

"Days of Een!" Kiro gasped, looking over his shoulder. "They're here! How do they move so fast?"

"SEE?" the door sneered, a gleeful observer of the memory. "They're going to take him, those Ungers! Watch now, child. Feel his fright!"

Kendra could feel it. Her heart was beating furiously. She wanted to help Kiro, to save him, the little helpless boy in the scene. But she could not. She was completely powerless. *No!* She screamed inside her mind. *How could I be so stupid? How could I have ever helped the very creatures who did this to poor Kiro? Never again...*

Hatred began to cloud her heart. She could feel it course through her body, unimpeded, like ink spilled in water.

"Goooood," the door chortled, as if he was watching her with voracious eyes.

Kendra felt her whole body beginning to transform into something ugly and wretched. She looked down at her hands and saw they were becoming deformed, like the claws of an Unger. She was becoming one of them. Yet, as this happened, the memory in her mind sped

forward; like a rock rolling down a hill, it could not be stopped. The memory had to play out.

So, even as she changed into an Unger, Kendra continued to see poor Kiro in her memory, waiting for the Ungers to snatch him. As an infant in the vision, Kendra could feel Kiro's hands shake as he held her. Then, at last, he placed her tiny body into a crack in the rocks, trying to hide her from the approaching beasts.

"Quiet now," he whispered bravely. "Not a peep! Okay, Little Star?"

But it was too late. The Ungers were there. With their rough claws they tore him away, forever. She squeezed her eyes shut and wailed. Then she felt the Ungers lifting her out of the crack. They tore open her blanket and glared at her with triumphant eyes. Then suddenly their expressions changed to confusion, then to fear. They had noticed something. She could see the terror on their craggy faces. It was her palm. They had seen the mark of the star.

"The forbidden onezum!" they screamed.

They dropped her to the ground and, just like that, they were gone. She was left all alone amidst the wilderness, a baby on a ledge of rock, and there she would lie until Uncle Griffin-skitch would discover her hours later. But now Kendra left the vision behind and returned to her eleven-year-old self. Her mind was reeling with the last words her brother had ever said to her: "Little Star."

This struck her. *Kiro was not the only one to have called me that,* she thought.

"Don't worry about it!" the door snapped, sensing her struggle. "It was your brother! That's what he used to call you."

No, Kendra thought. *Someone else.*

"Who else?" the door demanded. "Who else other than your brother would call you that?"

"Youzum right," Kendra declared, shocked at the sound of her voice, now changed into that of an Unger. "Only brotherzum."

"Yes . . . the last thing he said before they took him," the door snarled. "Those monsters. Those Ungers."

The Ungers, Kendra thought. *That's right. Kiro IS the only one to ever call me that.*

And then, in one moment of clarity, everything suddenly made sense.

Trooogul.

He was Kiro.

Kiro was Trooogul.

He was her brother.

He had been transformed into an Unger, all those years ago—just like she was turning into one at this very moment. There were no monsters in this maze at all. Uncle Griffin-

232

skitch, Oki, herself—all of them—they *were* the monsters. They had all transformed into the very things they loathed.

And now, something else happened. She was changing again. It was like she was coming to the surface of the water, as if she had been drowning and now suddenly had been thrust to the top, finally able to breathe again.

Kendra rubbed her eyes. She looked down at her hands. They were Een hands again. The transformation had stopped. She was still herself.

She looked about and found herself in a new room in the maze, one she had not yet been to. She wasn't sure how she had come to this place, but it was lighter and warmer here. Then she noticed that in the middle of this room, there was a low dais, and on the dais were the shattered remains of a cauldron. She could not be sure what had caused the destruction of the cauldron; but she did know whatever accident had befallen it had happened long ago, for its many fragments were old and rusted. Now the shattered remains of the cauldron seemed to glow, and rising forth from them was an apparition, cold and white and translucent.

"Who are you?" Kendra asked in bewilderment.

"I am the first Elder of Een," the ghost replied solemnly.

CHAPTER 29

The First Elder of Een

TO Kendra, the ghost's face looked just like the Door to Unger. It was his voice that was different, for it was no longer angry or threatening. If anything, Kendra felt that it was a hollow voice, sad and forlorn.

"Where am I?" Kendra asked.

"You have arrived at the center of the maze," the ghost replied. "Here the heart is darkest. Few have made it this deep—and then, only to succumb to their own hatred. But no longer will this be the case. Now there will be light, now that you have come."

"What are you talking about?" Kendra asked. "I don't understand. Why are you here?"

"This is my place," the ghost responded with a sweeping gesture of his hand, though there was not the slightest hint of pride in his voice. "This is the map of my dark heart. For of all Eens, I am the one who first felt hatred. Long ago, in the Days of Een, all were one, all were kind, and there was goodness in the land. And there were seven original Elders of Een, and I was the very first of all of them. We were not only seven Elders, we were seven brothers. And we watched over the Eens, with goodness in our hearts and in our minds. But there came a time when one Elder hungered for power over all others."

"It was you," Kendra declared. "The Wizard Greeve."

"Aye," the ghost said. "And my heart grew dark and twisted and poisoned, and I told myself that the other Elders, my brothers, would take the power if I didn't. So I decided to have it for myself."

"But they discovered your plot and banished you."

"You know the tale, I see," the ghost of Greeve murmured.

Kendra nodded. She wanted to be angry with him, but somehow she could not. Whatever anger she had felt, only a few moments before, had now evaporated—and it wasn't as if the wizard was real. He was just a ghost now, sad and pitiful.

"Then you know what happened next," the ghost continued. "After I was banished by my brothers, I traveled into the wilderness, my heart still seething with anger. And when I came here I built this temple with its dark door, so that it might corrupt all who enter it. I became this place, you know. I locked my soul and spirit into the wall, the very rock, so that I might live forever. Still, in this haven, I was able to trick my foolish brothers. They came here in hopes to make peace with me, but once I had them within the depths of my maze I cursed them, my brethren. Alas, one escaped my curse, my

brother Longbraids. He fled back to Een, hiding himself and his people from my wicked ways. But the others, they have been cursed every since."

"How can that be?" Kendra asked. "What do you mean? Aren't your brothers all dead and gone now?"

"The curse lives on, generation after generation," the great white ghost explained. "It has lived in this place, years untold. The Unger Keepers, they know the truth of the door. That is why they gather the beasts here each year, to honor the anniversary of that first curse and to cast any they have captured through the door. They thought they might conquer the Eens, one by one . . . so that one day your race would be made extinct."

"They would transform all of us into . . . into monsters," Kendra said.

"Aye," the ghost of Greeve said solemnly. "But you, my child, were able to break the curse."

"Because of Trooogul," Kendra said. "Because I discovered he is my brother."

"Not exactly," the ghost said. "You forged a friendship with Trooogul long before you learned his true identity—and that's what gave you the ability to destroy the curse. You felt fellowship, kindness and faith towards Trooogul when others of your kind could only fumble with emotions of mistrust and hate. Your belief in friendship with Trooogul allowed you to discover that he is your brother—but more importantly, it allowed you to break through the dark shroud of my heart."

"What happens next?" Kendra asked.

"The darkness lifts," the wizard replied solemnly. "The maze—my black heart—is shattered. Now, you must go . . . leave the maze, and return to your world."

"What will become of you?" Kendra asked, giving her braids a nervous tug.

"My dear, I am already dead," the ghost explained. "I bound myself to this maze long ago, so that the treachery of my heart could live on in this cold place. But you have destroyed my domain, and now my spirit will finally be released."

"But wait!" Kendra called. "How do I break the curse?"

"It shall not be undone," the ghost said gravely. "The curse is forgotten."

"There has to be a way," Kendra urged. "Tell me more! Tell about your brothers, the other Elders."

"There is no time," the ghost of Greeve declared, raising a white translucent finger. "Look, a light is shining; the temple is shattered."

Kendra turned around slowly, and now she noticed a ray of light beaming into the room from one of the passageways—but only one.

"The light will show you the path to the maze's exit," the ghost explained. "Now, step into the light! Return to your true selves!"

At first Kendra didn't understand what the ghost meant, for she had already turned back to her true self. Then she realized that she was no longer alone in the center of the maze with the apparition; six hideous creatures had entered and were now standing behind her. It was almost as if they had been beckoned. Some of the creatures Kendra recognized: the Orrid and Unger who had chased her and the Izzard who she thought had devoured Oki. But now that she knew the truth, she was no longer afraid of them. She watched with anticipation as the six beasts stepped into the light, and instantly their monstrous forms melted away—and there her companions stood.

"Kendra!" Oki exclaimed and she felt her heart leap with relief and joy. The little mouse rushed forward and Kendra hugged him so hard that he squeaked.

She would have embraced them all—but there was suddenly no time. The ghost was fading away and the entire maze began to tremble. The floor beneath them began to rupture and suddenly plants and trees began to spring forth, ripping up the stones with their roots and leaves. In other areas, water bubbled up through the rock, creating rivers across the floor of the maze.

"Time to leave!" Jinx declared.

"Whatever you do, stay in the light while we're in this maze," Kendra told them. "Otherwise you'll be transformed back into the creatures you were!"

Everyone stepped in line behind Jinx, save for Effryn, who seemed to be lingering by the broken remains of the cauldron.

"Hurry now!" Jinx commanded.

"Don't get your wings in a knot," the plump Faun replied. "I'm coming."

As soon as he had joined the group, Jinx hopped forward, following the path of light through the maze. As they left the hub of the maze, Kendra looked over her should, but the ghost of Greeve was gone and a jungle of life was sprouting up from where the remains of the cauldron had rested. Many of the trees had already ripped through the roof of the chamber, and now brilliant sunshine was flooding the place. The dark temple of the Wizard Greeve would soon be no more.

Quickly Jinx led them down the passageway, into the glaring ray of light. There were still many turns and twists in the maze, but the light showed them the way. Then, they turned a corner and standing before them was a young Een man, basking in the light. He wasn't wearing any clothes, save for a ragged pair of trousers. Even his feet were bare. Jinx came to an abrupt halt.

"Where did you come from?" she demanded.

The Een looked upon the small, bewildered party and flashed a white smile. He seemed about seventeen years old, tall and strong and handsome. But it was his eyes that Kendra noticed, for somehow she knew them.

"I'll be shorn!" Effryn piped up, for it seemed he had recognized those eyes too. "It's Trooogul, isn't it?"

"Not exactly," Kendra said. "It's—,"

"Kiro!" Uncle Griffinskitch exclaimed. "My boy!"

The old wizard hobbled forward, Kendra right on his heels, and together they were swept up in the young Een's arms. Kendra felt as if her heart would burst with joy. Her brother! At last she had found him, the real him; and, if she had found him, that meant she could find her parents too. Anything and everything seemed possible in that moment. Kendra was hungry, beaten, and exhausted—but she had never felt so exhilarated.

"My word!" Professor Bumblebean gasped. "Whatever is going on here?"

"There's no time to explain," Kendra said as Kiro finally released her from his embrace. "We better get out of here before there's nothing left of this place."

Jinx nodded and bounded ahead, taking the lead. The rest followed again, and this time Kendra, Kiro, and Uncle Griffinskitch took up the rear, all holding hands.

"How did you find us?" Kendra asked her brother as they scrambled through the crumbling wreckage of the maze.

"I heard you scream, Little Star," Kiro answered. "All the way from out there. Once the maze started to fall apart, I found a way in. It so happened I stepped into this light and, well—here I am!"

"It makes sense now," Kendra beamed. "All of it."

"Yes," Kiro said. "That old Unger Oroook was right all along. The Door to Unger showed us the truth."

"What about our parents?" Kendra said. "Do you know where they are?"

Kiro shook his head grimly. "I don't know what became of them, Kendra. Maybe they went through the door, just like me. Maybe not. I just can't remember."

Kendra felt her Uncle's hand on her shoulder. "We'll find them yet," the old Een declared.

They now had to focus all of their concentration on escaping the maze, for the way was becoming increasingly perilous. Stones were tumbling down from the high walls and ceiling in greater frequency, and this made the shaft of light more and more difficult to follow. Not only did they have to dodge the raining rocks, but many of the stones had fallen onto the path to impede their way.

"We're almost there!" Jinx hollered in encouragement as she hopped to the top of one such obstacle. "I can see the end."

With new vigor, the tiny grasshopper bounded ahead, the rest of the party close behind her. A gateway appeared before them and through it Kendra could see the Greeven Wastes stretch into the horizon—and yet, it was a wasteland no longer. The stadium had vanished, the monsters scattered, and the jumble of rocks was no more; for now it was replaced by lush forest and fields of wild flowers.

Kendra had never seen such a pleasant sight!

"We've made it," she murmured.

Jinx hopped through the door, and the others followed. Kendra, Kiro, and Uncle Griffinskitch were only a few paces away from the exit when suddenly a dark shadow loomed in the door, blocking their way. Kendra felt her heart skip. It was a cluster of creatures: a Goojun, a Krake, and one very ornery Unger.

"Creeegun!" Kendra gasped.

CHAPTER 30

A Brave Sacrifice

Kendra shook her head in confusion. "I don't understand," she said. "Why hasn't the light transformed them?"

"They can't change," Kiro murmured in reply. "They were born as Ungers and such. The light can't reverse that."

Kendra clung tightly to Kiro and Uncle Griffinskitch and wished more than ever that the old wizard had not lost his staff. Without it, they had no way to get past Creeegun and his cohorts.

Where's Jinx anyway? she asked herself angrily, but she realized that it was probably impossible to return to the maze after exiting it. So she stood there, alongside her brother and uncle, momentarily frozen in fear.

The temple continued to fall down around them. Now entire sections of the walls around the door gave way and collapsed to the ground. Before long, they no longer felt as if they were standing in a passageway, but rather just in the shaft of light that had guided them through the maze. On either side of them was a flat expanse of churning rock and jungle. Because of this, there were many directions to run—but Kendra could see that all avenues of escape would lead them out of the light—and that meant transforming back into monsters.

As for Creeegun, he did not seem the least bit perplexed by the tumbling stones or the quaking floor. He paced before the three Eens, his eyes wide and cruel. Behind him, the Goojun and Krake hovered, drooling.

"Wherezum Trooogul!?" Creeegun demanded.

"I'm Trooogul," Kiro announced, stepping in front of Kendra and Uncle Griffinskitch and letting go of their hands.

"Wherezum Trooogul!?" Creeegun repeated. "Seezum Trooogul enter mazeum—but nozum come outzum."

"I AM Trooogul!" Kiro uttered. "The maze changed me into an Een—my true self!"

This seemed too much for Creeegun and the other creatures to comprehend. They stared at Kiro with baffled expressions. As far as they were concerned, Kiro might as well have just announced that he was moving to the moon.

"We're not so different, you and I," Kiro told Creeegun. "Eens and Ungers, that is."

"LIAR!" Creeegun roared. "Trooogul betray Ungers, friendzum of Eeneez. But youzum! Youzum still killzum Trooogul."

"That's not true!" Kendra cried. "We didn't hurt him! He's right here!"

But now Creeegun had no interest in talking. "Killz them!" he spat, and he leapt forward with his fellows at his side.

Kendra shrieked. The Goojun was coming straight towards her, but at the last moment one of the falling rocks struck the reptilian creature and he crashed to the floor, unconscious at her feet. Creeegun plowed towards Kiro, but the young Een ducked beneath the Unger, escaping the rake of his claws. Uncle Griffinskitch was not so lucky; the Krake hit him with full force, bowling him to the ground and sinking its sharp fangs into his shoulder. The old wizard screamed in pain, and in the next instant Kiro was at his side, hurling a large rock at the Krake to knock him away.

"Kiro, look out!" Kendra cried, for now Creeegun had turned around and was charging at him again.

Kiro threw a wild, excited look in Kendra's direction. "Get Uncle Griffinskitch out of here!" he yelled, turning and running towards the edge of the light.

"What are you doing?" Kendra yelled. "Don't leave the light!"

But even as she spoke these words, Kiro leapt from the glowing path, into the flattened expanse beyond. Instantly, he was transformed into the large and grotesque form of Trooogul the Unger.

"NO!" Kendra screamed.

Creeegun, who had been rushing straight towards Kiro, now skidded to a halt, his large tusked mouth dropping open in amazement.

"Nowzum!" Trooogul growled, glaring at Creeegun and the Krake in triumph. "Youzum fightzum ME!"

It took a moment for Creeegun and the Krake to gather their wits. One minute they had been attacking an Een and in the next an Unger! But Kendra could see that they were both enraged, and the thing most important to them now was a fight. The Krake, who was actually the closest to Trooogul, made the first move by baring his sharp fangs and leaping at the Unger. Trooogul grunted and, with a swat of his mighty claw, batted the smaller creature away as if it was nothing more than a bug. The Krake struck the ground with a squeal and then lay in a motionless, crumpled heap. Now it was Creeegun's turn. He lowered his rocky head and charged forward. He hit his former friend square in the chest, but Trooogul instantly regained his feet and the two young Ungers were soon embroiled in a vicious battle on the expanse of rock that lay beyond the path of light.

"Gozum!" Trooogul roared at Kendra over the din of the fight and the collapsing maze. "Gozum, Little Star!"

He spoke with such authority that Kendra felt compelled to obey. She turned her attention to Uncle Griffinskitch, who was lying on the ground moaning in pain. She put her hands underneath each arm and pulled the old man across the quaking ground, through the door, and to the outside world. Just as they crossed the threshold of the door, the remainder of the temple came toppling to the ground, sending out a cloud of dust and rubble that knocked Kendra right from her feet. The last thing she was able to do before blacking out was to scramble on top of her uncle's body, to protect him from the debris that was raining down from the obliterated temple.

When Kendra returned to consciousness, the air had cleared and the sun was beaming kindly upon the land—it was the warmest she had felt in weeks. She coughed and felt the grainy taste of grit in her mouth. She looked down at herself and noticed she was covered head to foot in dust and grime. Then she blinked her eyes a few times and realized her friends were all hovering around her.

"Are you okay?" Ratchet asked her.

Kendra nodded and looked about, trying to gather in her surroundings. After all the noise of the temple's destruction, the world seemed incredibly quiet. Nearby, she could see a pile of rock and stone; it was all that was left of the temple maze and the Door to Unger—but Kendra knew it would not remain like that for long, for a tangle of trees and bushes were already sprouting forth from it in earnest. She turned her head and noted the sound of a brook and the aroma of wild meadow flowers. Everything had returned to life in the formerly wretched land.

Then Kendra remembered what had happened just before the final collapse of the temple.

"Kiro!" she murmured worriedly. "And Uncle Griffin-skitch! Where are they?"

"There's no sign of Kiro," Jinx said gravely, helping Kendra to her feet. "Your uncle is here, but he's in bad shape."

The old wizard was lying on the grass, mumbling incoherently. Kendra knelt beside him and stroked his forehead, now beaded with perspiration.

"Will he be okay?" she asked.

"Something bit him on the shoulder," Professor Bumblebean said. "What was it?"

"A Krake," Kendra sniffled.

"Brush my brow!" Effryn exclaimed, hobbling forward. "I'll be shorn if there's anything more deadly than the venom of a Krake!"

"Don't you have something for him, Mr. Hagglehorn?" Kendra asked the little Faun.

"No," Effryn replied sadly. "There's only one thing I know that can save someone from Krake venom—and that's the nectar of a fireflower. But I've never seen a fireflower; why, I'm not sure they even exist. Baste my beard, but I don't know where to find them."

Kendra smiled sadly down at her uncle. "I do," she murmured quietly.

CHAPTER 31

A Whisper Is Given

Kendra knew that she had to get Uncle Griffinskitch back to the land of Een as quickly as possible for it was there, and only there, that the fireflower grew. According to Effryn (and further supported by Professor Bumblebean) the Krake venom would claim the life of the old wizard if they did not get him the antidote soon.

As such, they needed to leave straight away—which meant there was little time to search for Kiro. They spent a few hours scouring the forest that was now growing from the wreckage of the maze, but there was no sign of Kendra's brother.

"What do you think became of him?" Oki wondered.

"He didn't die," Kendra declared. "That much I know."

"How?" Oki asked.

"I don't know," Kendra replied. "It's just a feeling."

"Well, your feelings have always served you well," Ratchet told Kendra. "If that's the way you feel, then you trust it. I think you'll be seeing Kiro again before you know it."

Kendra smiled. Somehow, Ratchet always knew the right thing to say to make her feel better.

"Do you think Kiro is still an Unger?" Jinx asked. "Or did he transform back into an Een again?"

"I don't know," Kendra said. "But either way, he's my brother."

"Come now," Professor Bumblebean said gently. "We need to leave, Kendra, if we are to save your uncle."

They set on their way. The first thing that needed to happen was for Effryn to find where he had hidden Skeezle. This was not an easy task, for when he had left the tiny snail it had

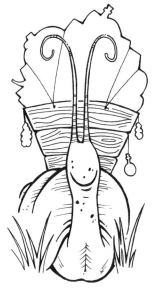

been at the edge of a barren wasteland—but now everything was lush and green. But find him Effryn did and at once he enacted his magic to enlarge the snail, along with his great collection of miraculous marvels.

"We'll let your uncle ride on Skeezle's back, in the carriage," Effryn told Kendra. "And I have a few medicines that may ease his pain and slow down the spread of the venom—so hopefully, we'll get him back to Een in time."

"Thank you, Mr. Hagglehorn," Kendra said.

As they headed towards the land of Een, Kendra looked over her shoulder to gaze upon the former wasteland one last time. For a moment she thought she saw the distant silhouette of Trooogul standing amidst the forest trees and she let out a gasp. But a moment later the silhouette was gone.

"Are you all right?" Jinx asked her, upon hearing her gasp.

"Yes, thank you," Kendra said turning to the grasshopper. "Let's hurry on."

Had she just imagined seeing the great Unger? She wasn't sure, but it made her feel better to think that she had.

I will see him again, she told herself. *I know it. There's a connection between us, that much is sure.*

The small band traveled hard for the next few weeks, stopping only to rest and gather food. Uncle Griffinskitch never spoke once during this journey. His health declined steadily, and Kendra fretted continually that he might die before they could reach Een. Thankfully, now that summer had arrived, the weather was warm and the skies were clear, allowing them to make good speed. At last, they reached the edge of Een.

"Home sweet home," Oki sighed happily as they came upon the magic curtain.

"Well, come on, my apprentice," Ratchet said. "In we go."

He plowed ahead, expecting to step easily through the magic curtain—but he did not! Instead it was like walking into a wall of rock, and the hapless raccoon fell straight onto his rump.

"What's going on?" Kendra asked worriedly. "As Eens, we should be able to walk straight through the curtain!"

"Oh my!" Professor Bumblebean exclaimed. "How could we forget? Burdock Brown sealed the magic curtain before we left. There's no way to get through!"

"But we have to!" Kendra exclaimed. "We need to get Uncle Griffinskitch into Een. He's not going to last much longer."

"This is outrageous!" Jinx snarled. "Why, I'd love to get my hands on that Burdock. Who does he think he is, keeping us out of our own land?"

"I can get you through," Effryn declared suddenly, and with these words, he produced the small silver bottle—the very one that contained the secret spell for opening the magic curtain.

"But I thought you wanted to sell it to the Elders," Kendra said to the Faun.

"Indeed," Effryn returned. "But I've had a change of heart, Kendra, or I'll be shorn. If not for you, I'd have never escaped that dreadful maze. Why, it's the least I can do, to give you this whisper."

"Thank you, Mr. Hagglehorn," Kendra said, taking the bottle from the Faun.

She removed the cap, put it to her ear, and listened to the spell.

"Did you hear it?" Oki asked anxiously after the girl had replaced the cap.

Kendra nodded. She turned to the curtain and repeated the incantation that she had heard. The curtain was invisible of course, but once she had spoken the enchantment the air in front of her seemed to shimmer—and Kendra knew that the curtain had parted for her.

At last, they were home.

CHAPTER 32

The Carvings in the Stone

Kendra sat on the sprouting stool in Winter Woodsong's cluttered room and welcomed the warm sunshine that was beaming through the open window. It had been three weeks since the girl and her companions had returned to Een, but it had not been until today that she had been able to leave the house and come to Faun's End. This was due to Uncle Griffinskitch; for even though the nectar of the fireflower had saved his life, the old wizard was still very weak and Kendra had been very busy nursing him back to health.

Now that her uncle was on the mend, Kendra had taken the opportunity to visit Winter Woodsong. Professor Bumblebean had related all of their adventures to the old sorceress, but Kendra knew Winter would want to see her in person. So here she sat, watching the ancient woman as she bustled about in the corner of the chamber, making some dandelion tea.

"You certainly look livelier, Elder Woodsong, since the last time I saw you," Kendra commented, not sure what else to say. She still felt uncomfortable around the old sorceress, especially when it was just the two of them alone.

"You're kind to say so," Winter said, shuffling up with a cup of tea for her.

"Will you return to the council, then?" Kendra asked.

"No, I'm afraid not," Winter replied. The old woman found a stool and with a wave of her staff cleared it of a pile of books so that she could sit down next to Kendra. "Burdock Brown rules the Elders now," Winter explained. "He would never allow me to take my seat, for he knows I would oppose him on so many of these cruel things he is trying to do."

"Someone needs to stop him," Kendra blurted.

"Indeed!" Winter agreed. "But it will not be me. No, I prefer the solitude of my chamber these days. I guess it comes with old age. If only the fireflower would cure *that!* But I'm glad to hear, child, that the flower has helped your uncle recover."

"Yes," Kendra said, taking a sip of her tea. "He's almost his old self again."

"Which means a lot of 'humphing,' I suppose," Winter said, a twinkle in her eye.

"I suppose," Kendra said with a laugh.

For a time they sat there quietly, drinking their tea. It always seemed to be that way with Winter, Kendra realized.

You could sit for several minutes with the old woman, without a word being said.

Then finally, Winter spoke. "Well, it seems you have solved the mystery of what became of your family," she commented.

"Many questions have been answered," Kendra said forlornly, "but still I have no family."

"Ah, but you do," Winter said. "They're just not with you at this moment."

Kendra nodded and absent-mindedly reached into her pocket to toy with her brother's compass. She carried the compass with her everywhere now; just having it next to her made her feel better somehow. It was like having a tiny piece of Kiro with her.

"Is something on your mind?" Winter asked.

"Yes, ma'am," Kendra said after a moment. "It's . . . well, it's about my brother. What if Kiro is still an Unger? And what if my parents are too? Is there any way to change them back, now that the door has been destroyed?"

"I'm afraid I don't know," Winter replied. "The Door to Unger has been closed forever. That is a good thing, for it means no Een will ever know its curse again. But for those who still carry the curse? Well, we can only hope there is a way to bring them home one day."

"I'm determined to find my family," Kendra told her. "I suppose there will be another journey for me, yet."

Winter chuckled, her face crinkling with wrinkles. "Child, I think there will be many journeys for you ahead. I'm afraid you're just not the stay-at-home type. You're too much like your mother."

Kendra smiled and found herself gazing upon the stone carving above Winter's bed. It had only been two months since Kendra had last seen the picture, but somehow it seemed like years.

"The scene looks different to me now," Kendra remarked.

"How so?" Winter asked.

"Before I thought I saw a great battle between Eens and Ungers and the other monsters," Kendra replied.

"And now?"

"I don't know," Kendra said. "It's almost as if . . . as if somehow the figures are all dancing together. Isn't it strange that it seems so different to me now?"

"Ah, such is the magic of art," Winter said, a twinkle in her old eyes. "You think the art has changed, but it has not at all, child. It has remained exactly the same."

"Then what is it?" Kendra wondered.

"Why, it's you, child!" Winter remarked with a merry laugh. "The change has been in *you*."

The
End

The Door to Unger

Drawn By Professor Broon Bumblebean

Cartographer's Note:
This map should not be viewed as
an accurate representation of the
temple maze of the Wizard Greeve.

All information is based solely on
personal experiences and conversations with
Kendra Kandlestar and other members
on the quest who were forced to enter the
treacherous labyrinth.

Many entered the maze, but not all returned.

Unger

Goojun

The Path of Light

Where the memory began

Crumbling Wall

Old Unger

Where Kendra knew the truth

Window

The heart of the MAZE

Izzard

Krake

Orrid

Where Kendra started in the maze

Oki

Orook's Chair

(now vacant)

The Door to UNGER

The Keepers

THE AUDITORIUM - where the creatures watch the Festival of Greeve

Kendra Kandlestar will be back!

Visit www.kendrakandlestar.com for all the latest Een news and to send your comments and feedback to Lee Edward Födi.

Readers Respond to Kendra Kandlestar

"I love your book Kendra Kandlestar and the Box of Whispers! It is the best book I have ever read! My favorite characters are Jinx, Kendra and Oki! Kendra because she is kind, thinks for herself and of others too! Jinx because she has courage, muscle and, best of all, power. I wish I was her. Oki is a very funny character since he always thinks about onions. I will read this book a lot in my lifetime."

~ Carmen, age 10

"I just finished this book! It's a great one too! Seeing that I finished, I now know my favorite characters! My most favorite character is Kendra Kandlestar for facing her fears, having hope, and being mischievous! But my other favorite character is Honest Oki, for his fears, and for once not being such the Honest Oki that he is! My next favorite character is Elder/ Uncle Gregor Griffinskitch for his magicalness (I don't think 'Magicalness' is a word!) and his everlasting 'Humphs'!"

~ Joshua, age 11

"I really really enjoyed Kendra Kandlestar And The Box of Whispers. My favorite part of the story was the end where they were in the dragon's castle . . . I really enjoy your books!"

~ Alanah, age 9

"Kendra Kandlestar and the Door to Unger left me in a lot of suspense; I could see the pictures in my head—and you find out so much more in The Door to Unger. It's awesome! It makes you kind of think."

~ Lucy, age 7

"I like Kendra Kandlestar so much that I don't know what to say."

~ Bayla, age 5

"I'm in grade four, I've read all of the books that you wrote. Kendra Kandlestar and the Box of Whispers is one of the best books I've read in my whole entire life, in fact our whole school thinks it's a great book. My whole entire class read it and chose it for our favorite book. I'm a big fan of yours, I'm waiting for the second book. I hope that you will write a third and fourth book, about Kendra and the gang. "

~Kay Zhu, age 9

"Our class read your book Kendra Kandlestar and the Box of Whispers and I really enjoyed it. I think that it's really descriptive and exciting. My favorite character is Oki. 'EEEK!'...please write a sequel."

~ Sandra, age 10

"Kendra Kandlestar is a magnificent book. Nothing is expected except for monsters around every twist and turn. I love Kendra, Oki, Griffinskitch, and Jinx. This is the best book ever made in the fantasy section. We all learn lessons from this book."

~ Matthew, age 11

"I like Kendra Kandlestar because she is adventurous, and she teaches us to be not afraid and she also has the courage to stand up for herself. I like Uncle Griffinskitch because in the book he tells us the right thing to do and even though he is grumpy in the book I believe he is only like that to protect Kendra. I like Honest Oki because he is honest, and at the end of the book even though he is scared he tried his best just to help Kendra. He is also a great friend to Kendra; he helps Kendra with a lot of things. I like professor Bumblebean because he is smart and I wish I was smart as him too. I like Jinx because she is strong and she is not afraid to try."

~ Mariel, age 11

"I really like your book Kendra Kandlestar and the Box of Whispers. It is the best! First, I thought when my teacher was going to read it, it was just a book because she said she had good news and I said what are the good news, I really want to know, but when she showed us the cover page I was just so surprised. I said to myself it's not just a book it's a magical book . . . I really like your book now I can't stop reading your book."

~ Ysabel, age 10

"My teacher finished your book, AND IT WAS AWE-SOME! My favorite part was when the orb chose Kendra and Oki to go on the adventure. I loved your book!"

~ Kristyn, age 10

"When I picked Kendra Kandlestar up there was practically no way I could put it down. It was a great book . . . I made a poem. It goes like this:

Kendra Kandlestar in the Lands of Een.

In search of the box of whispers for only few have seen.

Yet she stands and waits for mystery to unveil

As she tries to find the box, with secrets that will reveal."

~ Michael, age 8

"Kendra Kandlestar and the Box of Whispers was a really great mystery for the gang to get the Box of Whispers back from the Red Thief. I really liked it when Kendra and Oki worked to get the box . . . This is the BEST book I have ever read. EVER. And I read a lot of books. My momma says I have a mini library in my room. Hope there are more Kendra stories to come."

~ Haylee, age 11

"Your writing is phenomenal as well as your drawing. The part I liked in your book was when Kendra saved the little Unger. It reminded me of me when I help people out. I also like the Captain Jinx . . . I am your number 1 fan of your new book. Fantasy is one of my favorite types of books. To me it also sounds like mystery. I like it because I like secrets. I also like your drawings. I liked Uncle Griffinskitch."

~ Madison, age 11

"Dear Lee Edward Fodi, Wizard of Words . . . this book, I have tons to say. But they can be described in one word: Fantastic. Today, I would like to talk about Oki. (I liked that little mouse's name since it fits the picture on the front page.) Oki, I think, is a very funny mouse, even though he doesn't intend it. The funniest thing about him is the onion. Even though the same joke of 'don't think of onions' lasted all book long, it was so funny that every time it was mentioned, it made me grab my belly and roll. The mouse is so cute because with a little talking from Captain Jinx, it 'eeks', and I can imagine that sound."

~ Peter, age 13

"This book is special, because it has unusual things like the Riddle Door and the Garden of Books. I like Jinx, because she calls Professor Bumblebean funny names. I like the pumpkins, because they make stupid remarks. The book was good, because it was really funny. My favorite character was Captain Jinx, because she was funny but stern."

~ Bethany, age 8

"I love that book . . . I was so excited to finish it. I wish there was a part two. My favorite character is Kendra. My favorite part is when Oki turned into a giant onion! That was so funny."

~ Charlotte, age 9

"I loved your book! This is what I had to say about Uncle Griffinskitch: Uncle Griffinskitch is sometimes grumpy and says 'Humph' a lot and he is sometimes kind, because he forgave Kendra that she saved an Unger. He said if Kendra leaves Een so does he.

"I think Uncle Griffinskitch is great because he teaches us to forgive people for their mistakes."

~ Agnes, age 10

"Our teacher read us the book about Kendra Kandlestar. The book was great. I liked the part when Kendra helped everybody how she opened the box of whispers. I mostly liked Kendra Kandlestar and Oki."

~ Simran, age 9

"I read Kendra Kandlestar and the Box of Whispers. It was great! My favorite part is when Kendra goes inside the box and sees all the vials of secrets."

~ Dustin, age 10

"This book I could not put down! I think you should make a sequel, Mr. Fodi! And the drawings give them character too! I liked it when all the whispers came out of the box! It was enchanting! Please write another book! PLEASE write a sequel! THANKS FOR WRITING IT!"

~ Dona, age 10

"I love the variation of mythical and magical creatures. It's funny and full of surprises every step of the way, just like Artemis Fowl but better."

~ James, age 10

"I love magic, so I loved Kendra Kandlestar and the Box of Whispers. It had lots of excitement and action!"

~ Joyce, age 9

"I loved your book Kendra Kandlestar and the Box of Whispers. Our class is doing a novel study on your fantastic book! My favorite characters are Rumor, Jinx and Kendra. I like Rumor because is a dragon that breathes fire and have cool red scales. I like Kendra because she thinks for herself but not of herself. I like Jinx because she is brave and never gives up fighting. I liked how you came up with the Land of Een. It is one of a kind I will read your book at least ten times in my lifetime!"

~ Annie, age 9

Lee Edward Födi has been writing and illustrating stories about magic, monsters, and mystery for as long as he can remember. Growing up on a farm, he was subjected to various horrible chores such as cleaning up after chickens, pigs, geese, and younger siblings. Once, he was even accidentally locked inside the chicken coop. It's probably this incident that gave him the idea for writing *Kendra Kandlestar and the Door to Unger*, a story in which there are numerous doors, but none that harbor anything behind them quite so terrible as chicken dung. Födi now lives in Vancouver, Canada, and likes to stay as far away as possible from all farms.

Find out more at www.leefodi.com.